JACK LONDON'S

DEAR READER,

What's better than reading a great book? Reading one where you make the choices! I've loved choose your path books since I was in fifth grade, and I'm excited to share one with you now. But this isn't just any old story; it's a unique retelling of one of my favorite books.

So many of the stories I read as a child were choose your path books. And when I ran out of those, I read dog books. The first I remember devouring time and again was Jim Kjelgaard's *Wild Trek*, a survival story about a trapper and his pet. I was also fond of Jack O'Brien's *Silver Chief* series of dog books. But of course, in my opinion, *The Call of the Wild* was the best of them all.

Jack London's classic adventure is ripe with life-or-death situations. I have taken great care to keep much of London's own writing intact. But please consider this book a shortened introduction to *The Call of the Wild*.

When you reach a time, now or in the future, where it is appropriate for you to do so, I encourage you to read *The Call of the Wild* in its entirety. For now, I hope this version of the story will do.

—Ryan Jacobson

TABLE OF CONTENTS

HOW TO USE THIS BOOK

As you read *Jack London's Call of the Wild*, you will sometimes be asked to jump to a distant page. Please follow these instructions. Sometimes you will be asked to choose between two or more options. Decide which you feel is best, and go to the corresponding page. (Be careful; some of the options will lead you to disaster.) Finally, if a page offers no instructions or choices, turn to the next page.

Please, respect all wildlife and nature. Enjoy the story, and good luck!

DOG-SLEDDING TERMS

Canvas covering: a tarp put over a sled's cargo to keep items from falling out

Gee-pole: a pole attached to the front of the sled, allowing drivers to pull and guide it

Harness: a set of straps that connects dogs to a sled

Lash: the flexible material at the end of a whip

Lead dog: the dog at the front of a team; usually a strong and intelligent leader

Miners' meeting: a meeting in which a disagreement is decided by local residents

Runners: the narrow strips of ski-like wood beneath a sled, on which the sled glides over snow and ice

Sled lashings: ropes used to hold a sled together and to help keep cargo in place

Toil: very hard work

Traces: the parts of a harness that attach to a dog

Wheeler: the dog at the back of the team and right in front of the sled; often the heaviest dog

PROLOGUE: AN ACCIDENT

"I hate nature!" you shout. Of course, that's not true, but right now it feels like it. You have been saving your money for more than two months. You almost have enough to buy the new *Zombie Surfers* video game.

But now your dad is making you go on a camping trip. If that's not bad enough, he's making you pay for half of the sleeping bag you'll need. So it's bye, bye money—and bye, bye video game.

"I don't wanna go camping!" you yell.

You're so mad you can feel your cheeks getting hot. You spin away from your father, not waiting for him to respond. You want to throw something. Kick something. Scream something.

As you stomp up the stairs to your room, it's a bad time for the family dog, Lucy, to get in your way. The golden retriever wags her shaggy tail, panting happily as she trots down the steps toward you.

You've never really been much of a dog person. Your memories flash to times when Lucy jumped on you, scratched you, chewed your favorite toys—and now you want her gone.

She stops in your path, almost tripping you. It fills you with a momentary rage. You yell, "Get out of my way, Lucy! You're a bad dog!"

You aren't a mean person, and what happens next is an accident. But that doesn't make you feel any better.

Lucy cowers away from you, her head and her tail sagging. She steps on a book that you left on the stairs. It slides, and Lucy loses her footing. She rolls against the side of the stairwell and then tumbles down the five steps behind you.

Thump. Thump. Thump. Thump. Thump.

At the bottom, the dog skids to a stop. She whimpers softly as she staggers to her feet. It looks like she's going to be okay.

But Lucy has fallen hard and loud. It's enough to bring your dad running.

"What happened?" he exclaims. "Are you—" He looks up at you, down at Lucy, then up at you again. His wide, worried eyes morph into narrow slits of anger.

"What did you do?" he growls.

"It was accident," you whine.

He points up the stairs and shouts more loudly than you've ever heard him before. "Get to your room! I don't want to see you until morning."

You don't know what to do. You don't know what to say. So you lash out. "I'm never going camping with you!" You turn and run up the stairs to your room, slamming the door behind you.

As you lie in bed, wishing you were anywhere but here, you suddenly notice the muffled sounds of dogs barking and people yelling. The noise is faint at first, but it steadily grows louder. Strangely, it doesn't seem to be coming from outside or even downstairs. It's coming from your bookshelf.

You climb out of bed and creep toward the sound. It leads you to the bottom shelf, lined with crumbly, old books that you've never seen before: *The Adventures of Sherlock Holmes*, *Dracula*, *Treasure Island* and more. But the sounds seem to be coming from one book in particular: Jack London's *The Call of the Wild*.

You're afraid to guess what will happen if you pick up the book, yet you can't help feeling curious. Could this be the thrill of a lifetime? Will it be dangerous? Is there a chance you'll get hurt—or even killed?

You feel strangely certain that the answer is "yes" to all of the above.

The sound slowly begins to fade. Your instincts tell you it's now or never. You must decide, and you must decide fast. Will you pick up the book, or will you leave it be? What will you choose to do?

To pick up the book, turn to page 35.

To leave the book alone, turn to page 51.

As you draw yourself together to spring after the others, you see Spitz rush upon you. Once off your feet and under that mass of huskies, there will be no hope for you. But you brace yourself to the shock of Spitz's charge, then join the retreat out on the lake.

The nine team-dogs gather together and seek shelter in the forest. Dub is badly injured in a hind leg. Dolly, the last husky added to the team, has a badly torn throat. Joe has a scratched eye. Billee, with an ear chewed up, cries and whimpers throughout the night.

Turn to the next page.

At daybreak you limp back to camp. The invaders are gone, and the two men are in bad tempers. Half their food supply is eaten. The huskies have also chewed through the sled lashings and canvas coverings. They have eaten a pair of Perrault's moose-hide moccasins, chunks out of the leather traces, and even two feet of lash from Francois's whip.

After two hours of work, the harnesses are into shape. The wounded team is soon under way, struggling painfully over the hardest part of the trail yet. The river is wide open. Six days of exhausting toil are required to cover the next 30 terrible miles. And they are indeed terrible. Every foot of progress is accomplished at the risk of life to dog and man.

A dozen times, Perrault falls through the ice, being saved by the long pole he carries. However, a cold snap is on. The thermometer registers 50 below zero. Each time he breaks through, he must build a fire and dry his wet garments.

Once, the sled breaks through along with Dave and you. You are half-frozen and all but drowned by the time you are dragged out. The usual fire is necessary to save you. You are coated with ice, and the two men keep you on the run around the fire—so close that you are singed by the flames.

At another time, Spitz goes through, dragging two dogs after him. You watch him sink into the frigid waters, and you realize that this is your chance: You can be rid of your enemy once and for all. Every day he lives is another opportunity for him to attack. Sooner or later, he may gain the upper hand.

If you don't pull him out of the water, he will surely die. But he is the lead dog, and your team is already weakened. Part of you wonders if you can survive without him on the team. Should you pull Spitz out? Or should you let him drown? What will you choose to do?

To let Spitz drown, turn to page 62.

To pull Spitz out, turn to page 54.

14

You have avoided trouble with your enemy, and you will continue to do so—at least for now.

Tired and cold, you turn and march away from Spitz. Yet you should have guessed the bully would see this as a sign of weakness. Before you realize what is happening, Spitz leaps upon you and sinks his fangs into your left shoulder, cutting you deeply.

You tumble into the snow. The pain in your shoulder burns. You expect Spitz to pounce, to seize upon his advantage. He does not. Instead, it is the onlooking huskies who rush forward. All of them. They close in upon you, snarling and yelping. You are buried beneath them, stabbed by bite after terrible bite.

It does not take long. Two minutes from the time you went down, the pain subsides. You no longer feel the sting of teeth. You no longer feel anything. And as you breathe your last breath, you can at least be thankful that you're at peace.

Turn to page 73.

The night is too cold. Your only real option is to continue searching. You do just that, wandering until finally an idea comes to you. You return to see how your own teammates are surviving. To your astonishment, they have disappeared. Again you wander through the great camp, looking for them, and again you return. Where could they possibly be?

With drooping tail and shivering body, you circle the tent. The snow gives way beneath your fore legs, and you sink down. Something wriggles under your feet. You spring back, bristling and snarling, fearful of the unknown. But a friendly little yelp reassures you. A whiff of warm air fills your nostrils, and there, curled up under the snow, lies Billee. He squirms and wriggles to show his good will.

Another lesson. So that is the way they do it? You select a spot and dig a hole for yourself. The day has been long and difficult, and you sleep soundly and comfortably, though you growl and bark and wrestle with bad dreams.

Turn to the next page.

You awaken and bound straight up into the blinding day, the snow flying about you in a flashing cloud. Three more huskies have been added to the team, making a total of nine. Before another quarter of an hour passes, you are in harness and swinging up the trail.

You are glad to be gone, and though the work is hard, you find that you do not mind it. You are surprised at the change in Dave and Sol-leks. They are new dogs, transformed by the harness. They are alert and active, anxious that the work should go well. They become fiercely annoyed with whatever delays that work. Dave is wheeler, or sled dog. Pulling in front of him is you, and then comes Sol-leks. The rest of the team is strung out ahead, single file, to the leader, Spitz.

You have been placed between Dave and Sol-leks so that you might learn more. They never allow you to linger long in error, and they enforce their teaching with their sharp teeth. Dave is fair and very wise. He never nips you without cause, and he never fails to nip you when you stand in need of it. Francois's whip backs Dave up, so you find it better to mend your ways than to retaliate.

It is a hard run, across glaciers and snowdrifts hundreds of feet deep and over a great mountain, which stands between the ocean and the sad and lonely North. You make good time down the chain of lakes.

Late that night, you pull into a huge camp, where thousands of goldseekers reside. You make your hole in the snow and sleep. But all too early you are routed out in the cold darkness and harnessed with your mates to the sled.

The next day, and for many days to follow, you must make your own trail, work harder and move slowly. Perrault travels ahead of you, packing the snow with webbed shoes to make it easier for you.

Francois, guiding the sled, sometimes exchanges places with him, but not often. Perrault is in a hurry, and he prides himself on his knowledge of ice. The fall ice is very thin, and where there is swift water, there is no ice at all.

Day after day, you toil in the traces. Always, you awaken in the dark, and the first gray of dawn finds you hitting the trail anew. And always you pitch camp after dark, eating your bit of fish and crawling to sleep in the snow. A pound and a half of sun-dried salmon is your ration of food for each day, but it seems to go nowhere. You never have enough, and you suffer from unending hunger pangs.

Your mates, when finishing first, try to rob you of your unfinished ration. Food is energy in this harsh reality—and there isn't enough of either to go around. You cannot afford to miss a meal, but is it worth fighting about? Do you need to prove your dominance? Or should you join the others in stealing food? Which is the better way? What will you choose to do?

To fight to defend your food, turn to page 58.

To steal food for yourself, turn to page 50.

You draw yourself together. You prepare to spring, hair bristling, mouth foaming, a mad glitter in your eyes. Straight at the man you launch your 140 pounds of fury.

In mid air, just as your jaws are about to close on the man, you receive a shock that checks your body and brings your teeth together with an agonizing clip. You whirl over, hitting the ground on your back and side. You have never been struck by a club before.

With a snarl that is part bark and more scream, you again launch into the air. And again the shock comes. You are brought crushingly to the ground, but your madness knows no caution. A dozen times you charge, and each time the club breaks the charge and smashes you down.

After yet another fierce blow, you crawl to your feet. With a roar that is almost lion-like, you again hurl yourself at the man. He strikes a final blow, and you crumple up and go down, knocked senseless.

Turn to the next page.

Eventually, your senses come back to you, but not your strength. You lie where you fell, and from there you watch the man in the red sweater.

"Buck, my boy," he says, "we've had our little battle. The best thing we can do is to let it go at that. You've learned your place. I know mine. Be a good dog, and all will go well."

But have you learned your place? Are you ready to admit defeat? Or will you try once more to show the man in the red sweater what you're made of? What will you choose to do?

To attack the man again, turn to page 25.

To be a "good dog," turn to page 41.

Until now, you have avoided trouble with your enemy, but this is too much to bear The beast in you roars. You spring upon Spitz with a fury.

Spitz is equally willing. He cries with sheer rage and with eagerness as he circles back and forth for a chance to spring. You are no less eager and no less cautious. You likewise circle back and forth for the advantage. But it is then that the unexpected happens.

A shout from Perrault—the camp is suddenly alive with starving huskies, 40 or more of them, who have scented the camp. They have crept in while you and Spitz were fighting.

The two men spring upon the invaders with clubs, but the dogs show their teeth and fight back. They are crazed by the smell of food. Perrault finds one with its head buried in the grub-box. His club lands heavily on its lean ribs, and the grub-box spills upon the ground. Ten of the hungry brutes scramble for the bread and bacon. The clubs fall upon them, but they struggle madly until the last crumb has been devoured.

Your astonished team-dogs burst out of their nests only to be attacked by the fierce invaders. You have never seen such dogs. It seems as though their bones might burst through their skins. They are skeletons, draped loosely in dirty fur, with blazing eyes and fangs. But the hunger-madness makes them terrifying. There is no opposing them. Your team-dogs are swept back against the cliff.

You are attacked by three huskies. Your head and your shoulders are slashed. Billee is crying as usual. Dave and Sol-leks, with a score of wounds, fight bravely side by side. Joe snaps. His teeth close on the fore leg of a husky, a wise strategy. Pike leaps upon an animal.

You fling yourself onto an attacker. At the same time, you feel teeth sink into your throat. It is Spitz, treacherously attacking from the side.

Perrault and Francois hurry to save their sled-dogs. The wild wave of hungry beasts retreats before them, and you shake yourself free. But it is only for a moment. The two men must run back to save the grub, and the huskies return to their attack on you and your team.

Billee springs through the savage circle and flees over the ice. Pike and Dub follow on his heels, with the rest of the team behind.

This is your chance to escape as well, but is that what you wish to do? Run? You're still fighting mad. You could retreat with the others, or you could stay and defend your camp and your food. What will you choose to do?

To follow the other dogs, turn to page 12.

To stay and protect the camp, turn to page 36.

Refusing to admit defeat, you gather your strength, what little of it remains. Your muscles tense, and you spring forward in blur of rage.

Unlike your previous attacks, this one takes the man in the red sweater by surprise. Your teeth sink into his forearm and tear away his skin. You feel a moment of satisfaction as the man squeals in pain.

But the moment passes quickly. That final lunge stole the last of your energy. You're too weak to move as the man in the red sweater goes on the offensive. His club smashes down upon you, again and again. You fall to the ground and curl tightly into a ball. Still, the man doesn't stop.

"That's the last mistake you'll ever make," he cries.

You know he's right. Your body lies broken beyond repair. The pain has been replaced by a calming numbness. You wonder why it had to end like this, but the question doesn't long remain on your mind. Seconds after you ask it, the world around you fades to black. There are no more questions and no more answers.

Turn to page 73.

You drive in upon Spitz, shoulder to shoulder. You roll over and over in the powdery snow. Spitz gains his feet almost as though he has not been tackled. He slashes you down and leaps clear. Twice his teeth clip together, like the steel jaws of a trap. Then he backs away for better footing with a snarl.

The time has come. It is to the death. You circle about, ears laid back, watchful for the advantage. The other dogs have made short work of the rabbit. They are now drawn up in an expectant circle. To you, it is nothing new or strange, this scene of old time. It is as though it has always been the way of things.

Spitz is a practiced fighter. Bitter rage is his, but never blind rage. He never rushes until he is prepared to receive a rush.

You strive to sink your teeth into the big white dog. Wherever your fangs strike, they are countered by the fangs of Spitz. You cannot penetrate his guard. You warm up and envelope Spitz in a whirlwind of rushes. Time and time again you try for the snow-white throat, where life bubbles near to the surface. Each and every time, Spitz slashes you and gets away.

You take to rushing, as though for the throat. You draw back your head and curve in from the side, driving your shoulder at the shoulder of Spitz. You are a ram by which to overthrow him. Instead, your shoulder is slashed down each time, and Spitz leaps lightly away.

Spitz is untouched, while you are cut and panting hard. The silent and wolfish circle waits to finish off whichever of you goes down.

As you grow winded, Spitz takes to rushing. He keeps you staggering for footing. Once you fall over, and the whole circle of dogs starts up. But you recover yourself, and the circle sinks down again and waits.

You are losing this battle, and you are running out of time. You need a new strategy, and you must decide fast. Two areas on Spitz's body appear open to attack: his back and his legs. You must focus your next assault on one of those areas. What will you choose to do?

To attack Spitz's back, turn to page 52.

To attack Spitz's legs, turn to page 66.

I
INTO THE PRIMITIVE

If you could read newspapers, you would know that trouble is brewing, but you cannot read because you are a dog. Your name is Buck, and you are part Saint Bernard and part shepherd. You live at a big house in the sun-kissed Santa Clara Valley. Judge Miller's place, it is called. Here you have happily lived the four years of your life.

But now it is the fall of 1897. Men, groping in the Arctic darkness, have found gold. Thousands of men are rushing into the Northland. These men want dogs, and the dogs they want are heavy dogs, with strong muscles and furry coats to protect them from the frost.

Dogs like you.

Manuel, a gardener at Judge Miller's place, clamps a leash on your collar and takes you for a stroll through the orchard. No one notices you leave the big house, and only one man sees you arrive at the park. This man talks with Manuel, and money passes between them.

"You might wrap up the goods before you deliver him," the stranger says gruffly.

Manuel wraps a thick piece of rope around your neck, under the collar. "Twist it, and you'll choke him," he says.

You have learned to trust men in your four years as a dog. But when the ends of the rope are placed in the stranger's hands, your instincts warn you of trouble.

You growl.

To your surprise, the rope tightens around your neck, shutting off your breath. You spring at the man, but he is ready. He wrestles you close, and with a twist, throws you over on your back. The rope tightens again, and your strength fades. Your eyes glaze. You know nothing more, as you pass into sleep.

Turn to the next page.

You awaken, dimly aware that your tongue hurts. The loud shriek of a locomotive whistle tells you that you're inside a train.

You open your eyes, and you see the angry face of a dognapper. The man springs for you, but you are too quick. Your jaws close on his hand, and they do not relax until your senses are choked out of you again.

Dazed, suffering pain from throat and tongue, you feel your collar and the rope get removed. Your weary body is flung into a cage-like crate, where you spend a dreamless night.

For two days and nights you neither eat nor drink. You sometimes fling yourself against the bars, growling and barking, but it does no good. You do not mind the hunger so much, but the lack of water causes you a fever.

Four men carry the crate from the wagon into a small, high-walled backyard. A stout man with a red sweater comes out and signs the book for the driver. You hurl yourself savagely against the bars. The man smiles grimly and brings out a hatchet and a club.

"You ain't going to take him out now?" the driver asks nervously.

"Sure," the man replies, driving the hatchet into the crate.

The four men who carried the crate suddenly scatter. From safely on top of the wall they prepare to watch.

"Now, you little devil," the man says, when he has made an opening big enough for your body. At the same time, he drops the hatchet and shifts the club to his right hand.

You are cornered, trapped. The man with the red sweater stands between you and freedom. Can you get past him? Can you escape? Or will trying it be the last mistake of your life? What will you choose to do?

To attempt an escape, turn to page 20.

To stay in the cage, turn to page 56.

So far, you have avoided trouble with your enemy. You will continue to do so—for now. You will make a new nest.

Tired and cold, you turn and march away from Spitz. You should have guessed the bully would see this as a sign of weakness. Before you realize what is happening, you are under attack. Spitz leaps upon you and sinks his fangs into your left shoulder, cutting you deeply.

You tumble into the snow. The pain in your shoulder burns, but you won't stay down. You spring to your feet with a fury. But it is then that the unexpected happens.

A shout from Perrault—the camp is suddenly alive with starving huskies, 40 or more of them, who have scented the camp. They have crept in.

The two men spring upon the invaders with clubs, but the dogs show their teeth and fight back. They are crazed by the smell of food. Perrault finds one with its head buried in the grub-box. His club lands heavily on its lean ribs, and the grub-box spills upon the ground. Ten of the hungry brutes scramble for the bread and bacon. The clubs fall upon them, but they struggle madly until the last crumb has been devoured.

Your astonished team-dogs burst out of their nests only to be attacked by the fierce invaders. Never have you seen such dogs. It seems as though their bones might burst through their skins. They are skeletons, draped loosely in dirty fur, with blazing eyes and fangs. But the hunger-madness makes them terrifying. There is no opposing them. Your team-dogs are swept back against the cliff.

You are attacked by three huskies. Your head and your shoulders are slashed. Billee is crying as usual. Dave and Sol-leks, with a score of wounds, fight bravely side by side. Joe snaps. His teeth close on the fore leg of a husky. Pike leaps upon an animal.

You fling yourself onto an attacker. At the same time, you feel teeth sink into your throat. It is Spitz, treacherously attacking from the side.

Already injured from his first attack, you are in no shape to defend yourself. Spitz releases his grip on your throat and rushes you. He barrels you off your feet.

A moment later, a mass of huskies piles upon you. They close in, snarling and yelping. You are buried beneath them, stabbed by bite after terrible bite.

The final outcome does not take long. Two minutes from the time you went down, the pain subsides. You no longer feel the sting of teeth. You no longer feel anything. And as you breathe your last breath, you can at least be thankful that you're at peace.

Turn to page 73.

The decision is an easy one. Before the sound dies away, you quickly reach forward and snatch the book off the shelf. It feels rough and flimsy, like an old slice of bread.

As you pull the book toward you, the sounds grow louder again. The book wiggles in your hands, and you stare at it, gathering your courage. You take a deep breath, squeeze each end of the book and yank it open.

The room begins to spin. A wind starts to blow. Your bedroom grows black and cold. You feel your body being pulled downward. An invisible force pushes you closer to the pages before you. A sharp pain stabs at your forehead.

And then, suddenly, everything is still.

Turn to page 28.

It is not in your nature to retreat. While the rest of your team breaks away, you stand your ground. As you draw yourself together to prepare for an attack, out of the corner of your eye you see Spitz rush upon you. Once off your feet and under that mass of huskies, there will be no hope for you. But you brace yourself to the shock of Spitz's charge, then renew your fight with the starving invaders.

You ferociously tackle one of them. You leap onto another. No less than five of the brutes fall victim to your teeth before the others regroup. They quickly surround you. They outnumber you more than 20 to one. And yet you hold them at bay for several minutes.

You wait for the humans to come to your aid, but they must protect what food remains. The rest of your team—including Spitz—is gone. You stand alone.

The huskies are hungry, and their hunger makes them impatient. That would be to your advantage if there weren't so many of them. They attack like a swarm of bees, coming at you from all directions. You fight bravely, but you are quickly overwhelmed by their numbers. They bite and claw from all sides, and you are unable to defend yourself. Three, then five, then eight of the dogs pounce upon you, and you are driven to the ground.

The huskies close in, snarling and yelping. You are buried beneath them, stabbed by bite after terrible bite. Two minutes from the time you went down, the pain subsides. You no longer feel the sting of teeth. You no longer feel anything. And as you breathe your last breath, you can at least be thankful that you're at peace.

Turn to page 73.

You stand motionless, not daring to help. Curly is off her feet, and this is what the onlooking huskies were waiting for. They close in upon her, snarling and yelping. She is buried beneath the bristling mass of bodies.

You notice Spitz run out his tongue as if laughing. You see Francois and three other men swing clubs into the mess of dogs, to scatter them. It does not take long. Two minutes from the time Curly went down, the last of her attackers is clubbed off. But she lies there, lifeless.

So that is the way. No fair play. Once down, that is the end of you. Well, you will see to it that you never go down. Spitz runs out his tongue and laughs again, and from that moment you learn to hate him.

Before you have recovered from the shock caused by the tragic passing of Curly, you receive another shock. Francois fastens an arrangement of straps and buckles upon you and the other dogs. It is a harness.

You are set to work, hauling Francois on a sled into the forest to gather a load of firewood. You buckle down and do your best, though it is new and strange. Francois is stern, demanding obedience, and by use of his whip receiving it.

Dave, an experienced wheeler, nips your hind end whenever you make an error. Spitz is the leader. He growls at you or throws his weight to jerk you into the way you should go. You learn easily and make great progress. By the time you return to camp, you know enough to stop at "ho," to go ahead at "mush," to swing wide on the bends, and to keep clear of the wheeler when the loaded sled shoots downhill at your heels.

"Three very good dogs," Francois tells Perrault. "That Buck, he strong puller. I teach him quick as anything."

By afternoon, Perrault returns with two more dogs. Billee and Joe, two brothers and true huskies. They are as different as day and night. Billee has a good nature, while Joe is sour.

By evening Perrault has secured another dog, an old husky with a battle-scarred face and a single eye which commands respect. He is called Sol-leks, which means the Angry One. Like Dave, he asks for nothing, gives nothing, expects nothing. Even Spitz doesn't bully him.

As night falls, you face the great problem of sleeping. The tent, illuminated by a candle, glows warmly in the midst of the white plain. When you enter it, Perrault and Francois bombard you with cooking utensils. You flee to the outer cold. A chill wind nips you sharply and bites with venom. You lie down on the snow and attempt to sleep, but the frost soon drives you shivering to your feet. Miserable, you wander among the many tents, only to find that one place is as cold as another.

You don't know what to do. You cannot seem to escape the cold. You can continue to wander, hoping to discover a warm spot somewhere in this frigid world. But to do so will further sap your strength—and in these parts, a weak dog is a dead dog. Of course, if you don't find a warm place, you are in for a very long, uncomfortable night. Should you keep searching? Or should you lie down and rest where you are? What will you choose to do?

To continue searching, turn to page 16.

To lie down and rest, turn to page 53.

He fearlessly pats your head; you endure it without protest. When the man brings water, you drink eagerly. Later, you devour a generous meal of raw meat, chunk by chunk, from the man's hand.

You were beaten—but not broken. You saw, once and for all, that you stand no chance against a man with a club. You learned the lesson, and in all your life you'll never forgot it.

As the days go by, other dogs come in crates and at the ends of ropes. Now and again men come, strangers, who talk excitedly to the man in the red sweater. And when money passes between them, the strangers take one or more of the dogs away. You wonder where they go, for they never come back. And you are glad each time when you are not selected.

Yet one day, a little man who speaks broken English takes an interest in you.

"Wowee!" he cries, when his eyes lock upon you. "That one nice dog! Eh? How much?"

"Three hundred," replies the man in the red sweater. "It's a good price, eh, Perrault?"

Perrault grins. "He look like he one in a million."

You see money pass between them, and then you are led away by the little man. He takes another dog too: Curly, a good-natured Newfoundland. Perrault brings both of you to a large boat, where you are taken below and turned over to a black-faced goliath called Francois.

They seem like fair men, calm and wise. You feel certain that you are better off now than you were with the man in the red sweater.

You are soon joined by two other dogs. One of them is a big, snow-white fellow. He is friendly, in a sneaky sort of way. The other dog is a gloomy fellow, and he shows plainly that he desires to be left alone. "Dave" he is called, and he takes interest in nothing.

Day and night the ship throbs to the pulse of the propeller. It soon becomes apparent that the weather is growing colder. At last, one morning, the propeller is quiet, and the boat stops moving. You feel excitement in the air, and you know that a change is at hand.

Francois leashes you and brings you on deck. At the first step upon the cold surface, your feet sink into a white mushy something like mud. You spring back with a snort. More of this white stuff is falling through the air. You shake yourself, but more of it falls upon you.

You sniff it curiously, then lick some up. It bites like fire, and the next instant is gone.

You try it again, with the same result.

The onlookers laugh and say, "Look at that! It's Buck's first snow."

Turn to the next page.

2
THE LAW OF CLUB AND FANG

Your first day in this new place is a nightmare. Every hour is filled with shock and surprise. Every moment life and limb are in peril. There is a need to remain constantly alert, for these dogs and men are not town dogs and men. They are savages, all of them. They know no law but the law of club and fang.

You are camped near the store. Curly, in her friendly way, advances to Spitz, a husky dog the size of a grown wolf. There's no warning, only a leap in like a flash, a metallic clip of teeth. For no reason but meanness, the dog has bitten Curly's face from eye to jaw.

It is the wolf way of fighting, to strike and leap away; but there is more to it than this. Thirty or forty huskies run to the spot and surround the combatants in a silent circle. You do not understand the eager way they lick their chops.

Curly rushes her attacker, who strikes again and leaps aside. Spitz meets her next rush with his chest, tumbling her off her feet. Curly is outmatched.

She isn't exactly your friend, but you know Curly better than any of the other dogs—and she's in trouble. Should you help her? Or should you mind your own business? If you don't do something, Curly could get hurt, or worse. If you do step in, you might be the one who gets it. What will you choose to do?

If you choose to help Curly, turn to page 72.

If you choose to stay out of it, turn to page 38.

You've learned to trust your instincts. Right now, they're telling you not to tangle with a dog gone mad. Straight away you race. Dolly, panting and frothing, stays one leap behind.

You plunge through the woods and run down to the lower end. You cross a back channel filled with rough ice. You curve back to the main river and in desperation start to cross it. And all the time, you can hear Dolly snarling just one step back. Francois calls to you a quarter of a mile away, and you double back, still one leap ahead, gasping painfully for air. You shoot past Francois, and he puts the mad Dolly out of her misery with an axe.

Safe at last, you stagger against the sled. You are exhausted, sobbing for breath, helpless. This is Spitz's opportunity. He springs upon you. Twice his teeth sink into you. Francois's lash falls, and you watch as Spitz receive a whipping.

"One devil, that Spitz," remarks Perrault. "Some day he get that Buck."

"No, that Buck two devils," Francois answers.

You know that the clash for leadership will come. You want it because it is your nature. You have been gripped tight by pride—that pride which lures dogs to live joyfully in the harness and breaks their hearts if they are taken out of it.

In the days that follow, you interfere with Spitz's authority. There is constant bickering. Trouble is always afoot, and you are at the bottom of it. You keep Francois busy. On more than one night, the sounds of fighting among the other dogs awakens him. He rises, fearful that you and Spitz are at it.

You pull into a town called Dawson one dreary afternoon. Here are many men and countless dogs, and you find them all at work. They swing up and down the main street in long teams. In the night their jingling bells still go by. They haul cabin logs and firewood, and they do all manner of work that horses did in the Santa Clara Valley.

Turn to the next page.

Seven days from the time you pulled into Dawson, you pull back toward the ocean. The week's rest has recuperated the dogs, but the turmoil led by you has destroyed the unity of the team. No more is Spitz a leader to be feared. The dogs grow equal to challenging his authority. Pike robs him of half a fish one night; he gulps it down under your protection. Another night Dub and Joe fight Spitz. You never come near Spitz without snarling. In fact, you act much like a bully.

The breaking down of discipline also affects the dogs in their relations with one another. They quarrel and bicker more than ever. Francois stamps the snow in rage, and he tears at his hair. He knows you are behind the trouble, and you know he knows. But you are too clever to be caught red-handed. You work faithfully in the harness, for the toil has become a delight. Yet it is a greater delight to start a fight amongst your mates.

One night after supper, Dub turns up a snowshoe rabbit, blunders it, and misses. In a second the whole team and dogs from other teams are in full cry. The rabbit speeds down the river, turns off into a small creek. It runs lightly atop the snow, while you plow through by main strength. You lead the pack around bend after bend, but you cannot gain.

Straining after food that is alive and fleeing, you awaken the deeps of your nature. You feel a surge of life, the tidal wave of being. It is the perfect joy of each separate muscle, flexing under the stars.

You round the bend. You see a large animal leap from the overhanging bank into the path of the rabbit. It is Spitz. The rabbit cannot turn, and Spitz's white teeth bite into his prey. The pack raises a chorus of delight. But you do not cry out. You feel cheated of your game.

Spitz has interfered in your life once too often. Every fiber of your being tells you that the time for battle is now. Are you finally strong enough to defeat him? Or will picking a fight with Spitz end in your ruin? What will you choose to do?

To attack Spitz, turn to page 26.

To leave Spitz alone, turn to page 15.

Each night, it is the same. While you fight off two or three dogs, your fish disappears down the throats of others. You are left with no choice. Hunger compels you so greatly that you are not above taking what does not belong to you.

You watch and learn. When you see Pike, one of the new dogs, steal a slice of bacon when Perrault's back is turned, you duplicate the performance the following day. You get away with the whole chunk. A great uproar is raised, but you are not suspected. Dub, an awkward blunderer who is always getting caught, is punished for your misdeed.

It is all well enough in the Southland, under the law of love, to respect private property and personal feelings. But not in the Northland. Under the law of club and fang, whoever considers such things will fail.

A month ago, you would have died for the defense of Judge Miller. But you are no longer that dog. Now you look out only for yourself. The things you do are done because it is easier to do them than not to do them.

Turn to page 59.

You hesitate for moment, weighing your options. As the sound grows fainter, you decide that the risk is too great. You step away from the book and return to bed.

Even before your head hits the pillow, the peculiar noise is gone. Thank goodness. You close your eyes and try to clear your mind, but your anger continues to stir. Your dad, your dog, the whole world, you are mad at everyone and everything.

Some part of you, however, can't help but wonder if you've just missed a rare opportunity—one that might have changed your life forever.

"Oh, well," you tell yourself. "It's too late to think about that now."

You roll onto your side, pulling your blanket tightly around you. You feel certain that you will never be a "dog person." You'll never love the great outdoors either. And no matter what your dad says or does, you won't go camping with him. You'd much rather stay home and play your video games . . . unless, of course, he takes those away too.

Turn to page 73.

You fight by instinct, but you can fight by head as well. You rush, as though attempting the old shoulder trick. But at the last instant, you leap up toward Spitz's back. The bold maneuver exposes your underside. Your opponent seizes the opportunity. He strikes fast, ripping open your belly.

You yelp in pain. You have never experienced such agony. Yet, despite the mortal wound, you struggle madly to keep up.

The silent circle, with gleaming eyes, closes in. You stagger back and forth, snarling with horrible menace. Spitz springs in. His shoulder at last squarely meets yours. You fall off your feet and roll into the snow.

The onlooking huskies rush forward. All of them. They close in upon you, snarling and yelping. You are buried beneath them—trampled, bitten and scratched.

The end comes quickly. Within two minutes' time, all of your pain fades away. Your body grows numb. Your breathing slows. You close your eyes and exhale one final time. Your journey is at an end.

Turn to page 73.

You are cold and alone. Your strength is leaving you rapidly. It is unwise to continue wasting it, wandering around the camp.

You consider the spot where you stand. It is as good as any other. You let your body drop into the frigid, wet snow, and you wrap yourself tightly together.

For several long hours, the wind and blowing snow slap against you, pricking you like 1,000 tiny needles. Eventually your body numbs to the pain. You feel a deep longing for sleep. Your weariness is so great that you know you could not fully awaken, if you wished to.

Your eyes grow heavy, and your breathing becomes slow and rhythmic. Your body relaxes, even as the cold overwhelms you.

You force your eyes open once more, taking in the lonely wintery scene before you. And then you close your eyes a final time. Your body comes to rest, as you drift into a sleep from which you will never awaken.

Turn to page 73.

You cannot allow Spitz to die, for you realize that you are about to be pulled into freezing water too. You strain backward with all your strength, your fore paws on the slippery edge and the ice snapping all around. Behind you, Dave likewise strains. And behind the sled is Francois, pulling until his muscles crack.

By the time you make it to good ice, you are tired out. The rest of the dogs are too, but Perrault pushes you late and early. All day long you limp in agony, and when camp is made, you lay down like a dead dog.

Hungry as you are, you will not move to receive your fish. Francois must bring it to you. He also rubs your feet for half an hour each night after supper. And he sacrifices the tops of his own moccasins to make four moccasins for you. This is a great relief for a time, but eventually your feet grow hard to the trail. The worn-out footgear is thrown away.

Turn to the next page.

One morning, as you are harnessing up, Dolly breaks into a long, heartbreaking wolf howl. It sends every dog bristling with fear. Then she springs straight for you. You have never seen a dog go mad, yet you know that here is horror.

You are smarter, stronger and a much better fighter than Dolly. Yet something deep within tells you to run. Should you trust your instincts? Should you retreat, showing weakness and fear in front of your mates? Or should you stand your ground? What will you choose to do?

To stand your ground, turn to page 64.

To run from Dolly, turn to page 46.

You have been choked and caged. Your throat and tongue throb with pain. You are hungry and with fever. There is no fight left in you.

The man in the red sweater clutches his club tightly. He looks ready for battle, but you will not give him the satisfaction. You slink into the far corner and wearily plop to the floor. A soft whimper escapes your lips.

The man reaches his club into the crate and pokes you sharply in the ribs. You do your best to ignore it. He repeats his performance. Again you pay him no regard.

The man in the red sweater turns away from you and shouts toward the wall. "What did you do to him? The dog has no spirit!"

The men sitting there shrug and scratch their heads. "He wasn't like that before," one of them offers.

The man in the red sweater stares back at you, and he spits. He pauses for a long moment and then finally sighs. "The dog is worthless," he says. "Get rid of him."

You remain in the corner as the four men climb down from the wall. You sit motionless as the largest of them slips another rope around your neck. You do not protest as the men lead you away from the crate.

They walk you far from that backyard, deep into some unknown forest. There, the large one releases his hold of the rope, and the men hurry away, leaving you to fend for yourself.

You collapse to the ground and press your eyes closed. Away from the Santa Clara Valley, your world has lost all meaning. You have no reason to carry on. What will you do now? Where will you go? The answer escapes you, for you do not yet understand your true nature. And because of that, you will live the rest of your life lost and alone.

Turn to page 73.

Try as you might, there is no defending it. While you fight off two or three, your fish disappears down the throats of the others. To remedy this, you eat as fast as they.

It is all well enough in the Southland, under the law of love, to respect private property and personal feelings. But not in the Northland. Under the law of club and fang, whoever considers such things will fail.

A month ago, you would have died for the defense of Judge Miller. But you are no longer that dog. Now, you look out only for yourself. The things you do are done because it is easier to do them than not to do them.

Turn to the next page.

Your muscles are as hard as iron. You are numb to ordinary pain. You can eat anything, no matter how disgusting. Sight and scent have become remarkably keen. Your hearing has developed well. Even in your sleep you hear the faintest sound. You have learned to bite out the ice with your teeth when it collects between your toes. When you are thirsty and when there is ice over the water hole, you break it with stiff fore legs. You can scent the wind and forecast the weather a full night in advance.

Not only do you learn by experience, but instincts come alive in you. It is a simple matter for you to learn to fight like a wolf. These skills come to you without effort, as though they have been yours always. And on the still cold nights, when you point your nose at a star and howl long and wolflike, it is your ancestors howling down through you.

Turn to the next page.

3
THE DOMINANT BEAST

The dominant beast is strong in you, and under the fierce conditions of trail life, it grows. You are too busy adjusting to the new life to feel at ease. You do not pick fights, and you avoid them whenever possible. You are not prone to rash behavior. In the bitter hatred between you and Spitz, you remain patient. On the other hand, Spitz never loses an opportunity of showing his teeth. He goes out of his way to bully you, trying to start the fight which could end only in the death of him or you.

Your team makes a miserable camp on the shore of a large lake. Driving snow, a wind that cuts like a hot knife, and darkness have forced your team to grope for a camping place. At your backs, a wall of rock rises.

Perrault and Francois must make their fire and spread their sleeping bags on the ice of the lake itself. They have discarded the tent in order to travel light.

Close beside the sheltering rock, you make your nest. It is so snug and warm that you hesitate to leave it when Francois distributes the fish. But when you finish your meal and return, you find your nest occupied. A warning snarl tells you that the trespasser is Spitz.

Is this the moment you have been waiting for? Is the time for battle now? Are you strong enough and skilled enough to defeat your enemy? Or should you allow him this victory and wait to fight another day? What will you choose to do?

To attack Spitz, turn to page 22.

To let Spitz have your nest, turn to page 32.

Finally, a chance to defeat your enemy—you intend to take it. You relax, allowing Spitz to sink farther and farther beneath the surface. But as he goes, so does the rest of the team. Too late, you realize your mistake. More dogs tumble into the frigid water, dragged forward by the harness that connects all of you to Spitz.

You are unwillingly pulled closer to the deadly hole in the ice. You dig your paws into the slippery edge. You push backward, straining with every muscle in your body. Behind you, Dave likewise strains. And behind the sled is Francois, pulling till his muscles crack.

Had you begun sooner, you may have been able to save the others and yourself. But now the forward momentum is too great. You are helplessly dragged into the freezing water.

You are greeted by a stabbing pain. The cold water bites like a million tiny insects. Your first instinct is to cry out, and as you do, you swallow a mouthful of the icy water. You fight to keep your head afloat. Yet any chance of survival ends when the sled plunges into the water behind you.

Your harness pulls tightly against you. You stretch your mouth and nose upward, struggling for one last gasp of air. The strain is too great. You are pulled to the bottom, where you struggle in vain to free yourself.

You hold your breath, still pushing upward with all of your might. But, too quickly, the last of your breath runs out. Panic and instinct take over. You inhale one final time. Your lungs fill with water, spelling the end of a short life. The river is now your final resting place.

Turn to page 73.

You are confident in your abilities as a fighter. You have nothing to fear. So you stand your ground.

Panting and frothing, Dolly is on you in one leap. Under normal conditions, you could take her down without much effort. But these conditions are anything but normal. Dolly is raving mad, and her attack is as ferocious as it is insane.

She bites and snaps with no regard for her safety. She scratches and claws, ignoring her injuries—as if she can not feel them. Her attack is without motive or strategy. Her wild and random movements leave you battered and confused.

Turn to the next page.

You stagger against the sled, exhausted, sobbing for breath. This is Spitz's opportunity. He springs upon you. Twice his teeth sink into you. Francois's lash falls, but it is too late. Dolly started the job; Spitz has finished it.

As the snow around you turns red, you begin to feel light-headed and dizzy. You see the world spinning, but it seems to be moving without you. Your surroundings fade out of focus, becoming a blur.

You close your eyes and stumble three steps forward. Then you collapse into the snow. There is no more pain. There is just the motionless, empty body of the dog you used to be.

Turn to page 73.

You possess a quality that makes for greatness: imagination. You fight by instinct, but you can fight by head as well. You rush, as though attempting the old shoulder trick. At the last instant, you sweep low to the snow and in. Your teeth close on Spitz's left fore leg. There is a crunch, and the white dog now faces you on three legs. You repeat the trick and break the right fore leg.

Spitz struggles to keep up. But the silent circle, with gleaming eyes and lolling tongues, closes in upon him. There is no hope for him.

You maneuver for the final rush. A pause seems to fall. Every animal is motionless as though turned to stone. Only Spitz quivers and bristles. He staggers back and forth, snarling with horrible menace.

You spring in, and your shoulder at last squarely meets his shoulder. You spring out, and the dark circle becomes a dot on the snow. Spitz disappears from view. You stand and look on, the successful champion, the dominant beast.

Turn to the next page.

4
WHO HAS WON TO MASTERSHIP

"What I say? I speak true when I say that Buck two devils." This is Francois's speech when he discovers Spitz missing and you covered with wounds. He draws you to the fire and by its light points them out.

Perrault surveys the gaping rips and cuts.

"And now we make good time," adds Francois. "No more Spitz, no more trouble, sure."

Perrault packs the camp and loads the sled. Francois proceeds to harness the dogs. You trot up to the place Spitz would have occupied as leader, but Francois brings Sol-leks to the position. In his judgment, Sol-leks must be the best lead-dog left.

You spring upon Sol-leks in a fury, driving him back and standing in his place.

"Eh?" Francois cries, slapping his thighs gleefully. "Look at Buck. Him think to take Spitz's job. Go way!"

You refuse to budge.

Francois becomes angry. "Now, I fix you!" he cries. He comes at you with a heavy club in his hand.

Remembering the man in the red sweater, you retreat slowly. Sol-leks is once more brought forward. The driver goes about his work. He calls to you when he is ready to put you in your old place in front of Dave. You retreat two or three steps. Francois follows; you again retreat.

Perrault and Francois run you about for the better part of an hour. They throw clubs at you. You dodge and answer with snarls, keeping out of their reach. You do not try to run away, but you retreat around and around the camp. When your desire is met, you will come in and be good.

Perrault looks at his watch. Francois shakes his head and grins sheepishly at his companion, who shrugs his shoulders in sign that they are beaten. Then Francois goes up to where Sol-leks stands and calls to you. He unfastens Sol-leks' traces, and he puts him back in his old place.

There is no place for you but the front. You trot in, laughing triumphantly, and you swing around into position at the head of the team.

At a bound you take up the duties of leadership. Where judgment is required, and quick thinking, you show yourself the superior even of Spitz. But it is in giving the law and making your mates live up to it, that you excel.

The general tone of the team picks up immediately. It recovers its old-time solidarity, and once more the dogs leap as one dog in the traces. At the river rapids, two huskies, Teek and Koona, are added. The speed with which you break them in takes away Francois's breath.

"Never such a dog as that Buck!" he cries. "Him worth one thousand dollar!"

The trail is in excellent condition, well packed and hard. There is no new-fallen snow with which to contend. It is not too cold. The men ride and run by turn, and the dogs are kept on the jump, making infrequent stops.

On the last night of the second week, you top a pass and drop down the sea slope. The lights of the city of Skaguay are at your feet. It is a record run.

For three days Perrault and Francois throw chests up and down the main street, while the team is the constant center of a worshipful crowd.

Next come official orders. Francois calls you to him, throws his arms around you, weeps over you. And that is the last of Francois and Perrault. Like other men, they pass out of your life for good.

A Scotch man takes charge of you and your mates. In the company of a dozen other dog-teams, he starts back over the weary trail to Dawson. It is no light running now. It is heavy toil each day, with a heavy load behind. This is the mail train, carrying word from the world to the men who seek gold under the shadow of the Pole.

You do not like it, but you bear up well to the work. One day is very like another. Each morning, fires are built, and breakfast is eaten. Then, while some people break camp, others harness the dogs. You are under way an hour or so before dawn pierces the darkness.

At night, camp is made, and the dogs are fed. To you, this is the best part of the day. After the fish is eaten, you loaf around for an hour or so with the dozens of other dogs. There are fierce fighters among them, but three battles with the fiercest brings you to mastery.

It is a hard trip, with the mail behind you, and the heavy work wears you down. You are short of weight and in poor condition when you arrive at Dawson. But in two days' time you are expected to drop down the Yukon bank, loaded with letters for the outside.

You should have a week's rest. You are in no shape for the journey, and neither are your mates. Another hard trek without sufficient rest could kill some or all of your team—even you. But do you dare disobey your new master? Should you refuse to leave? Or is doing so more dangerous than the journey itself? What will you choose to do?

To lead your team out of Dawson, turn to page 90.

To refuse to leave Dawson, turn to page 134.

You have seen enough. Before Spitz can renew his attack, you jump to Curly's aid. You land between her and her bully, and you growl menacingly. Spitz sneers at you, and the circle takes a step back.

You've never fought another dog before, but you can plainly see that you're bigger than he is. This gives you confidence. You charge Curly's attacker.

Just as he did with Curly, Spitz meets your rush with his chest. You thump against the surprisingly powerful dog, and you stumble backward. You fall off your feet, and you roll into the snow.

You expect Spitz to pounce, to seize his advantage. Instead, it is the onlooking huskies who rush forward. They close in upon you, snarling and yelping. You are buried beneath them, stabbed by bite after terrible bite.

It does not take long. Two minutes from the time you went down, the pain subsides. You no longer feel the sting of teeth. You no longer feel anything. As you breathe your last breath, you can at least be thankful that you're at peace.

Turn to the next page.

THE END

TRY AGAIN

Thornton doubts you. To be honest, you doubt yourself. But the thought of disappointing him is too much to bear. You slowly nod your head, as if to say yes.

Thornton smiles. He puts all two hundred dollars against six hundred from Matthewson. Your master's fate is in your hands now.

Matthewson's team of ten dogs is unhitched, and you are put in front of the sled. You have caught the excitement. Murmurs of admiration at your splendid appearance go up.

"Wow, sir!" stutters a wealthy observer. "I offer you eight hundred for him, sir, before the test, sir—eight hundred just as he stands."

Thornton shakes his head and steps to your side.

The crowd falls silent.

Thornton kneels down. He takes your head in his two hands and rests cheek on cheek. He whispers in your ear, "As you love me, Buck. As you love me."

You whine with eagerness. As Thornton gets to his feet, you seize his mittened hand between your jaws. You press in with your teeth and release slowly. It is the answer, in terms, not of speech, but of love.

Thornton steps well back. "Now, Buck. Gee!"

Thornton's voice rings out, sharp in the tense silence. You swing to the right, ending the movement with a sudden jerk of your 150 pounds. The load quivers, and a crisp crackling arises from under the runners.

"Haw!" Thornton commands.

You duplicate the maneuver, this time to the left. The crackling turns into a snapping. The sled pivots, and the runners slip and grate several inches to the side. The sled is broken out.

"Now, mush!"

Thornton's command cracks out like a pistol-shot. You throw yourself forward, tightening the traces with a jarring lunge. Your whole body is gathered compactly together in the tremendous effort. Your chest is low to the ground, your head forward and down. Your feet fly like mad, the claws scarring the hard-packed snow.

The sled sways and trembles, half-started forward. One of your feet slips, and a man groans aloud. Then the sled lurches ahead in a rapid succession of jerks. Half an inch. An inch. Two inches. The jerks diminish as the sled gains momentum, until it is moving steadily along.

Men gasp. Thornton runs behind, encouraging you with short, cheery words.

You draw near the pile of firewood, which marks the end of the hundred yards. A cheer begins to grow and grow, which bursts into a roar as you pass the firewood and halt.

Hats and mittens fly in the air—even Matthewson's. But Thornton falls on his knees beside you. Head against head, he shakes you back and forth.

"Wow, sir!" splutters the wealthy observer. "I'll give you a thousand for him, sir—two thousand, sir!"

Thornton rises to his feet. His eyes are wet. Tears stream down his cheeks. "No, sir," he replies. "He's not for sale."

You seize Thornton's hand in your teeth. Thornton shakes you back and forth. The onlookers draw back to a respectful distance and watch.

Turn to the next page.

7
THE SOUNDING OF THE CALL

Sixteen hundred dollars richer, John Thornton and Pete and Hans, with you and half a dozen other dogs, face into the East on an unknown trail. You sled 70 miles up the Yukon, threading the mountain peaks which mark the backbone of the continent.

Thornton is not afraid of the wild. He hunts his dinner during the day's travel. So, on this journey into the East, ammunition and tools make up the sled's entire load.

To you it is boundless delight, this hunting, fishing, and wandering through strange places. For weeks at a time you hold on steadily, day after day. For weeks upon end you camp, here and there, the dogs loafing and the men burning holes through frozen muck.

Looking for gold, they wash countless pans of dirt by the heat of the fire. Sometimes you go hungry; sometimes you feast, all according to the abundance of game and the fortune of hunting.

Summer arrives, and you raft across blue mountain lakes. You travel unknown rivers in slender boats built from the forest's trees. The months come and go. Back and forth you twist through the uncharted wild, where no other men are. You move across divides in summer blizzards. You shiver on mountains under the midnight sun. You drop into summer valleys amid swarming gnats and flies. And in the shadows of glaciers, you pick strawberries and flowers as ripe and fair as any the Southland can boast.

In the fall of the year, you reach a weird lake country. There is no life nor sign of life. There is only the blowing of chill winds, the forming of ice, and the rippling of waves on lonely beaches.

And through another winter, you wander on the trails of men who have gone before.

Spring comes again. At the end of your wandering, you find a shallow place in a valley. There, the gold shows like yellow butter across the bottom of the washing-pan. You search no farther.

Each day, the men earn thousands of dollars in clean dust and nuggets. The gold is sacked in moose-hide bags, 50 pounds to the bag, and piled like so much firewood. Like giants, the men toil. Days pass like dreams, as they heap the treasure up.

There is nothing for the dogs to do, so you spend long hours musing by the fire. A call within you sounds, as if from the depths of the forest. It fills you with a great unrest. You are aware of wild yearnings and stirrings.

Sometimes you pursue the call into the forest. You look for it as though it were a thing to find. You thrust your nose into the cool wood moss or into the black soil. You snort with joy at the earth smells. You crouch for hours behind trunks of fallen trees, studying all that moves and sounds about you. You do not know why you do these various things. You are compelled to do them.

Strong impulses seize you. You may be lying in camp, dozing lazily, when suddenly your head lifts. You spring to your feet and dash away, and on and on. You wander for hours, through the forest and across the open spaces.

You love to run and to creep and spy upon the bird life in the woods. For a day at a time, you will lie in the underbrush where you can watch partridges drumming and strutting.

But especially, you love to run in the dim twilight of the summer midnights. You listen to the sleepy murmurs of the forest; you seek the strange something within you that calls. It calls, waking or sleeping, at all times, for you to come.

One night, you spring from sleep with a start. You are eager, nostrils quivering and scenting, your mane bristling. From the forest comes a new call: a long-drawn howl unlike any noise made by dog. And yet you know it, in the old familiar way, as a sound heard before.

You spring through the camp and dash through the woods. As you draw closer to the cry, you go with more caution, until you come to an open place among the trees. Looking out, you see a long, lean timber wolf, its nose pointed to the sky.

Is the wolf friendly, or is he a foe? Is he alone, or is he the bait of a trap set by his pack? These thoughts and more race through your mind as you decide your next course of action. You do not wish to attack this beast, for you sense a kindred spirit. You would like to know the wolf better, but is it wise to approach it? Or will doing so bring you into battle against an entire pack of wolves? It's time to decide. What will you choose to do?

To leave the wolf, turn to page 104.

To approach the wolf, turn to page 135.

You make a dangerous, desperate decision. There is food to be had in other camps, and you intend to get it. You and your team need it, if you have any hope of surviving this journey. Dave proved that.

When darkness falls, you command the others to follow as you creep away from camp. The delicious smell of meat fills your nostrils. Your stomach pangs, and you know that this is the right choice.

Turn to the next page.

It takes more than two hours to reach the source of the smell, but you finally arrive at the edge of another team's camp. It is not unlike your own. The dogs sleep, buried in their underground beds. The men, two of them, are huddled beside a warm fire. Next to them sits a small stack of supplies, and there lies your target: a box full of food.

You pause for a moment, trying to devise a plan of attack. But hunger is a great motivator, and the rest of your team does not share your patience. They charge into the camp, straight toward the supply of food.

What happens next is an explosion of chaos. The men jump to their feet. One grabs a club, the other an axe. Their dogs leap out of the ground and attack your mates.

Even before the grub-box is reached, two of your dogs are downed—victims of the men and their weapons. An instant later, the camp's dogs are upon your team. They work in harmony with their human masters. They distract your comrades long enough for the men to finish them.

You run to the aid of your team, but this bout was lost the moment your dogs charged into camp. Even before you join the fight, all of the others are gone but Sol-leks. You leap to his side. Together, you battle bravely. No less than five dogs fall under your bites. You may even be able to take out the entire team, if not for their masters.

Beside you, you hear a deadening thunk, followed by a sharp yelp. And then Sol-leks is no more. You see a club flash toward you. For an instant, you remember the man in the red sweater. Then the club lands against your face, and you go down.

A mass of huskies piles upon you. They close in, snarling and yelping. You are buried beneath them, stabbed by bite after terrible bite.

The final outcome does not take long. Two minutes from the time you went down, the pain subsides. You no longer feel the sting of teeth. You no longer feel anything. And as you breathe your last breath, you can at least be thankful that you're at peace.

Turn to page 73.

You desperately wish to help John Thornton, but you know your limitations. The effort to save him would likely kill you. Unfortunately, he is on his own.

A large wave smashes against the rock. Your master disappears from view. The wave breaks, revealing the rock once more, but John Thornton is no longer there.

A long, heartbreaking howl escapes your lips. Your heart stings as if pierced by a sharp blade. Thornton can not, will not, last. He is dead, and you feel suddenly certain that you could have saved him.

The pain of his loss is so great that it drives you to the ground. You collapse into the sand, and you press your eyes closed. Your world has lost all meaning. You have no reason to carry on. What will you do now? Where will you go? The answer escapes you, for you do not yet understand your true nature. And because of that, you will live the rest of your life lost and alone.

Turn to page 73.

You're a skilled fighter. You can take down an adult moose. But even you are no match for an entire pack of wolves. And since you cannot defeat them, there is but one option: run.

You spin away from the predators and push hard against the ground. You launch yourself, running at full speed within seconds. In a straight race, you could probably outrun any wolf, but this is not a straight race. You know the forest well, and you maneuver quickly. But you were not born into it. You are not one with it, as the wolves are.

You dodge the trees, but the wolves almost seem to go through them. The obstacles in your path work against you. They slow you down—not much, but enough.

The wolves gain on you.

It doesn't happen quickly; you run for a long while. But eventually, the wolves overtake you. The fastest of them leaps upon your back, and you roll to the ground. In doing so, you twist your back leg. You will fight this battle on three legs.

You shrug off the first wolf, and a second attacks. He sinks his teeth into your side and then leaps away. As he jumps back, a third dashes in. Then a fourth. Then a fifth. Before you can begin a counter attack, your body is covered with bites and cuts.

On three legs, you are not as quick, and you are not as strong. The wolves attack together, fighting as one. In your weakened condition, you do not stand a chance. They pile upon you. They close in, snarling. You are buried beneath them—trampled, bitten and scratched.

The end comes quickly. Within two minutes' time, all of your pain fades away. Your body grows numb. Your breathing slows. You close your eyes and softly exhale one final time. Your journey is at an end.

Turn to page 73.

EPILOGUE:
A NEW CALL

You snap awake. You glance all around. You see your dresser, your bookshelf, dirty clothes scattered about the floor. You feel the warm comfort of your bed and a thick blanket wrapped around you. Sunlight creeps through your bedroom window, telling you that it's morning.

Was it all a dream? It doesn't seem like it. You feel oddly excited—like you can't wait to see what today brings. You think of camping with your dad, and you leap out of bed. You pull open your top dresser drawer and count the money piled in it. You wonder if you'll have enough to buy a fishing pole and a flashlight—after you pay for the sleeping bag.

And you won't forget Lucy. You want to buy her something nice. While you're at it, maybe you can even convince Dad to bring her on your trip.

You smile widely. "This is going to be great," you tell yourself. And then you hurry out of your room, eager to answer a new call, eager to see what adventures await you out in the wild.

Turn to page 120.

You remember the man in the red sweater. You know better than to disobey your master, so you decide to do as you're told. Far sooner than you should, you depart from Dawson.

You and your dogs are tired, the drivers grumbling, and to make matters worse, it snows every day. This means a soft trail, greater friction on the runners, and heavier pulling for you. Yet the drivers are fair through it all, and they do their best for the animals.

Each night the dogs are attended to first. You eat before the drivers eat. No man seeks his sleeping bag until he has seen to the feet of his dogs. Still, your strength weans down. Since the beginning of winter, you have traveled 1,800 miles, dragging sleds the whole weary distance. You stand it, keeping your mates up to their work, though you too are very tired. Billee cries in his sleep each night, Joe is sourer than ever, and Sol-leks is unapproachable.

But Dave suffers most of all. Something has gone wrong with him. Sometimes, he cries out in pain. The driver examines him but finds nothing. Something is wrong inside, but they can locate no broken bones.

Dave becomes so weak that he falls in the traces. The Scotch calls a halt and takes him out of the team. Sick as he is, Dave grunts and growls while the traces are unfastened. He whimpers when he sees Sol-leks moved to the position he has held so long. The pride of trace and trail is his. Dave cannot bear that another dog should do his work.

When the sled starts, he attacks Sol-leks with his teeth, rushing against him and trying to thrust him into the soft snow on the other side. Dave strives to leap inside his traces and get between Sol-leks and the sled. All the while, he whines and yelps and cries with grief and pain.

The Scotch tries to drive him away with the whip, but Dave pays no heed to the stinging lash. He refuses to run quietly on the trail behind the sled. He continues to flounder alongside, where the going is most difficult, until exhausted. Then he falls, howling as the long train of sleds churns by.

With the last of his strength, he manages to stagger along behind until the train makes another stop. He flounders past the sleds to his own, where he stands alongside Sol-leks. He pleads with his eyes to remain in his place there.

The driver and his comrades talk of how a dog can break its heart through being denied the work. So he is harnessed in again. Proudly he pulls as of old, though more than once he cries out from the pain of his inward hurt. Several times he falls down and is dragged in the traces. But he holds out until camp is reached.

Morning finds him too weak to travel. At harness-up time, he tries to crawl to his driver. He worms his way forward slowly toward where the harnesses are being put on his mates. His strength has left him, and the last time you see him, he is gasping in the snow and yearning toward you. You hear his mournfully howl until you pass out of sight behind a belt of river timber.

Here, the train is halted. The Scotch slowly retraces his steps to the camp. A revolver-shot rings out. The man comes back. The whips snap, and the sleds churn along the trail. But you know, and every dog knows, what took place behind those river trees.

Turn to the next page.

Each day of the journey steals more of your strength. You worry that Dave's fate may become yours, as well. You need energy, and the only way to get it is by finding more to eat.

Your memory turns to the starving huskies that once invaded your camp, and an idea forms in your mind. There is food to be had at other camps. Perhaps you should take it.

You and the rest of your team could sneak away, invade another site, eat your fill, and then get out of there. It could be just what you need to survive this journey. But, on the other hand, attacking another camp would be dangerous. Should you risk your life to find more food? Or will you gamble that you already have enough strength to finish this trip? What will you choose to do?

To invade another camp, turn to page 82.

To remain at your camp, turn to page 106.

You desperately wish to help John Thornton, but you know your limitations. The effort to save him would likely kill you. Unfortunately, he is on his own.

You watch helplessly as Thornton passes through a mad swirl of water, where the wild current goes wilder. He scrapes over a rock, bruises across a second, and strikes a third with crushing force. He clutches its slippery top with both of his hands.

A realization dawns on you, one that fills you with dread: A man can cling to a slippery rock in the face of a driving current for only a matter of minutes. John Thornton isn't going to survive. The waves pound him, one after another. His grip slowly loosens. His fingers slide apart.

A large wave smashes against the rock; your master disappears from view. The wave breaks, revealing the rock once more, but John Thornton is no longer there.

A long, heartbreaking howl escapes your lips. Your heart stings as if pierced by a sharp blade. John Thornton cannot, will not last. He is dead, and you feel suddenly certain that you could have saved him.

The pain of his loss is so great that it drives you to the ground. You collapse into the sand, and you press your eyes closed. Your world has lost all meaning. You have no reason to carry on. What will you do now? Where will you go? The answer escapes you, for you do not yet understand your true nature. And because of that, you will live the rest of your life lost and alone.

Turn to page 73.

You are not just a ferocious fighter, you are also a highly intelligent one. You are no match for an enraged, protective grizzly, and you know it. Fortunately, you are also fast and maneuverable. Escape is a simple matter.

You turn and run, using the trees to your advantage. The grizzly gives chase, but you dart to and fro. The forest's natural obstacles slow your attacker, and by the time you reach camp, the grizzly is gone.

You crawl into your den and lie down to sleep. You have wasted time and precious energy, but at least you are alive.

Turn to the next page.

It is a simple matter to give you and the other dogs less food, but it is impossible to make the dogs travel faster. Your masters do not know how to work dogs, and they do not know how to work themselves. Disaster is inevitable.

The first to go is Dub. His injured shoulder, left untreated and unrested, goes from bad to worse. Finally Hal puts the dog out of his misery. It is a saying of the country that an Outside dog starves on the ration of a husky. So your team's six Outside dogs can do no less than die on half the ration of a husky.

Mercedes ceases weeping over the dogs. Instead, she is occupied with weeping over herself and quarrelling with her husband and brother. Charles and Hal argue whenever given a chance. It is the cherished belief of each that he did more than his share of the work. Sometimes Mercedes sides with her husband, sometimes with her brother. The result is an unending family quarrel. In the meantime, the fire remains unbuilt, the camp half pitched, the dogs unfed.

Mercedes insists in riding on the sled. She weighs 120 pounds—a last straw to the load dragged by your weak and starving team. She rides for days, until you fall in the traces and the sled stands still. Charles and Hal beg her to get off and walk. On one occasion they lift her off the sled by force. They never do it again. She lets her legs go limp like a spoiled child, and she sits down on the trail. They go on their way, but she does not move. After you have traveled three miles, you must pull the sled back to get her.

In their own misery, they are cruel to you and your team. And through it all, you stagger along at the front. You pull when you can. When you can no longer pull, you fall down. You remain down till blows from a whip drive you to your feet again.

As it is with you, it is with your mates. There are seven all together, including you. In their misery, they have become numb to the bite of the lash and the bruise of the club. When a halt is made, they drop down in the traces like dead dogs. And when the club or whip falls upon them, they totter to their feet and stagger on.

Turn to the next page.

There comes a day when Billee, the good-natured, falls and cannot rise. You see it, and you know that this fate is very close for you. On the next day Koona goes, and just five of you remain: Joe, Pike, Sol-leks, Teek, and you.

It is beautiful spring weather, but neither dogs nor humans can enjoy it. From every hill slope comes the trickle of running water, the music of unseen fountains. All things are thawing, bending, snapping.

You stagger into John Thornton's camp at the mouth of a river. When the sled halts, you drop down as though you have been struck dead. Mercedes dries her eyes and looks at John Thornton. Charles sits on a log to rest. Hal talks. John Thornton whittles on an axe handle and listens.

"They told us the ice was melting—that the bottom was dropping out of the trail. They told us the best thing for us to do was to wait," Hal says. "They told us we couldn't make White River, and here we are." This last statement he sneers with a ring of triumph.

"And they told you true," John Thornton answers. "The bottom's likely to drop out at any moment. I tell you straight: I wouldn't risk my life on that ice for all the gold in Alaska."

"All the same, we'll continue on to Dawson," says Hal. He uncoils his whip. "Get up there, Buck! Mush!"

The whip flashes out, here and there. John Thornton bites his lips. Sol-leks is the first to crawl to his feet. Teek follows. Joe comes next, yelping with pain. Pike makes painful efforts. Twice he falls over but on the third attempt manages to rise.

Death is near; you can feel it in your bones. These masters are leading you to an end. Your instincts tell you to stay where you are, but you know what happens to dogs who don't follow orders. Do you dare disobey the humans? Are you willing to except the consequences? Or is it safer to do as you're told and continue on this journey? What will you choose to do?

To lead the team out of the camp, turn to page 122.

To refuse to leave the camp, turn to page 140.

A gust of overpowering rage sweeps over you. You growl aloud with a terrible ferocity. It is because of your great love for John Thornton that you lose control.

The Yeehats hear your fearful roar and see you rushing upon them. You are a live hurricane of fury, hurling yourself upon them in a frenzy. There is no stopping you. You plunge about in their midst, tearing, rending, destroying. In constant and terrific motion, you dodge the arrows they discharge at you.

A panic seizes the Yeehats. They flee in terror to the woods. You rage at their heels as they race away. The Yeehats scatter far and wide over the country. As for you, you return once more to the desolated camp.

Thornton's struggle is fresh-written on the earth, and you scent every detail of it down to the edge of a deep pool. By the edge lay Skeet, head and fore feet in the water. The pool itself, muddy and discolored, hides what it contains—and it contains John Thornton. You detect his scent into the water, from which no scent leads away.

John Thornton is dead. It leaves a great void in you, somewhat akin to hunger. It is a void which aches and aches and which food cannot fill.

Night comes on, and a full moon rises high over the trees into the sky. With the coming of the night, you become alive to a stirring of the new life in the forest. You stand up, listening and scenting. A faint, sharp yelp drifts from far away, followed by a chorus of similar sharp yelps. The yelps grow closer and louder.

Turn to the next page.

You walk to the center of an open space and listen. It is the call, the many-noted call, sounding more luring than ever before. And as never before, you are ready to obey. John Thornton is dead; the last tie is broken. Man and the claims of man no longer bind you.

Hunting their living meat, the wolf pack has at last crossed over from the land of streams and timber. They pour into the clearing where the moonlight streams, and in the center of the clearing you wait.

The wolves glare at you, making their intentions clear. They mean to attack. Are you strong enough to stand against an entire wolf pack? Or will doing so be the end of you? Is it wiser to escape, to ensure your lonely freedom elsewhere in this rugged land? Or will you stand your ground? What will you choose to do?

To run from the wolves, turn to page 86.

To stay where you are, turn to page 130.

A lone wolf is no match for you, but you do not trust that this wolf is alone. Approaching him might bring his entire pack upon you. Fortunately, the wolf is not yet aware of your presence; it is best to leave it that way. You turn around and start slowly back to camp.

For the better part of an hour, you hold steadily on your way. But before you reach your destination, your progress is interrupted. You happen upon a large grizzly bear, startling her and her cub.

The frightened bear's instincts are to protect her baby. This puts her into attack mode, leaving you with no choice. You are in for a battle. You growl low and guttural, and you bare your fangs.

The grizzly charges. At the last instant, you leap out of her path, slashing her side with your claws.

The grizzly whirls and again rushes. And again you do your trick, slashing her side a second time. You are quicker and wiser than your foe. Or so you think.

The grizzly charges a third time, but she has learned her lesson. This time, as you leap and slash, the bear reaches out with her massive paw. Speed is no match for strength. She swats, and you are flung backward.

You slam into a tree with the force of a moving car. You hear the bones in your back snap, and you bounce to the ground with a thud. When you try to push yourself up, you find that you cannot move.

The grizzly leaps upon you. You hear a frenzied snarl and see a flash of white teeth. But you feel no pain. You feel nothing at all. And as you close your eyes for the final time, you are grateful, at least, for that.

Turn to page 73.

Your team is weak, and invading another camp is no guarantee of food. Some or all of you could get hurt or killed. You decide that it's best to stay put.

You dig a den in the snow, and you try to make yourself comfortable. Your journey is a long one, and you'll need all the rest you can get.

Turn to the next page.

5

THE TOIL OF TRACE AND TRAIL

Thirty days from the time you leave Dawson, your team arrives back at Skaguay. You are worn out and worn down. Your 140 pounds have dwindled to 115. The rest of your mates are in no better shape.

Your feet fall heavily on the trail, jarring your body. There is nothing the matter with you except that you are dead tired. It is the dead-tiredness that comes through months of toil.

There is no power of recuperation left, no reserve strength to call upon. It has been all used, the last bit of it. In less than five months' time, you have traveled 2,500 miles. During the last 1,800 miles, you have had just five days' rest.

"Mush on, poor sore feets," the driver encourages. "This is the last. Then we get one long rest. For sure."

The drivers expect a long rest. But many men have rushed into the Klondike, and many wives have sent them letters. There are official orders. Fresh batches of Hudson Bay dogs are to take the places of those too tired for the trail. The tired ones are to be sold.

Three days pass. You and your mates find how really tired and weak you are. Then, on the morning of the fourth day, two men from the States come along and buy you, harness and all. The men address each other as "Hal" and "Charles." Charles is a middle-aged, light-ish-colored man. He has weak and watery eyes and a mustache. Hal is a youngster of 19 or 20, with a pistol and a hunting-knife strapped about his belt. Both men seem out of place in the North.

You see money pass between men, and you know that the Scotch and the mail-train drivers are passing out of your life. You are driven with your mates to the new owners' camp, and you find a mess: tent half stretched, dishes unwashed, everything in disorder.

You see a woman. "Mercedes" the men call her. She is Charles's wife and Hal's sister.

You watch as they take down the tent and load the sled. The tent is rolled into an awkward bundle three times too large. The dishes are packed away unwashed. Mercedes flutters in the way of her men. When they put a sack on the front of the sled, she suggests it should go on the back. When they put it on the back and cover it with other bundles, she discovers articles which must be placed in that very sack. So they unload again.

Three men from a neighboring tent come out and look on. They grin and wink at one another.

"You've got a load that's too heavy," says one of them. "Do you think it'll ride?"

Charles and Hal put the last odds and ends on top of the mountainous load.

"Why shouldn't it?" Charles demands shortly.

"It seems a mite top-heavy," the man replies.

"And the dogs can hike along all day with that behind them," adds a second of the men, mockingly.

"Certainly," says Hal. He swings his whip. "Mush!" he shouts. "Mush on there!"

You spring against your bands and strain hard, but you and your team are unable to move the sled.

"The lazy brutes, I'll show them," Hal cries.

"They're weak as water, if you want to know," says one of the men. "They need a rest."

Again Hal's whip falls upon you. You throw yourself against the bands. You get down low to it and put forth all your strength. The sled holds as though it is an anchor. After two efforts, you stand still, panting. The whip whistles savagely.

One of the onlookers speaks up. "It's not that I care a whoop what becomes of you. But for the dogs' sakes, I just want to tell you. You can help them by breaking out that sled. The runners are froze. Throw your weight against the gee-pole, right and left, and break it out."

A third attempt is made, this time following the advice. Hal breaks out the runners, which were frozen to the snow. The overloaded sled forges ahead. You and your mates struggle frantically under the rain of blows.

A hundred yards ahead, the path turns steeply into the main street. As you swing on the turn, the sled turns over—spilling half its load through loose lashings.

Kind-hearted citizens gather the scattered belongings. Also, they give advice: half the load and twice the dogs. Hal and his sister and brother-in-law listen. They pitch tent and overhaul the outfit. Canned goods are turned out. The tent and dishes are thrown away, as well.

Mercedes cries when her clothes-bags are dumped on the ground and thrown out. She cries in general, and she cries in particular over each discarded thing. Finally, wiping her eyes, she proceeds to cast out even articles of clothing that are needed. And when she finishes with her own, she attacks the belongings of her men. She goes through them like a tornado.

Even cut in half, the load is a heavy bulk. Charles and Hal go out and buy six Outside dogs. They bring the team up to 14 dogs total. But the Outside dogs do not amount to much. They do not seem to know anything. You and your comrades look upon them with disgust. And though you teach them their places and what not to do, you cannot teach them what to do.

The outlook is not bright. The men, however, seem quite cheerful and proud. They are doing the thing in style, with 14 dogs—more than anyone else!

Of course, there is a reason why 14 dogs should not drag one sled. One sled cannot carry enough food for 14 dogs. But Charles and Hal obviously do not know this.

Late next morning you lead the team up the street. You are exhausted before you start. Your heart is not in the work. You are without confidence in your masters. There is no depending upon these men or the woman. They do not know how to do anything, and as the days go by it becomes apparent that they cannot learn.

They are slack in all things. It takes them half the night to pitch a camp and half the morning to get the sled loaded. For the rest of the day, they are occupied in stopping and rearranging the load. Some days you do not make ten miles. On other days you are unable to get started at all.

Eventually, your team goes short on dog-food. Hal awakens one day to the fact that his dog-food is half gone and the distance only quarter covered. So he cuts down the ration and tries to increase the day's travel.

Turn to the next page.

Soon, hunger drives your every decision. You take to wandering alone at night, hoping to find a meal—a rabbit, a squirrel, anything.

You happen upon something even better. As you stalk through the frozen wasteland, you discover a creature that could fill your empty stomach eight times over: a stray bear cub. The baby grizzly appears lost and helpless.

Your muscles tense. Your stomach pangs. And your mouth begins to water. You leap into action, springing toward your prey with amazing speed. You are almost upon the cub, even before it is aware of your presence.

Turn to the next page.

A thunderous roar halts your progress. You spin quickly toward the noise and see a monstrous ball of fur and fangs rolling toward you. It is the cub's mother.

You are a dog without fear, a strong and cunning warrior. You need the meal this opportunity provides, and you long to test your strength against such a worthy foe. Yet there is no beast more dangerous than a mother defending her cub. Should you stay and fight? Or should you flee? What will you choose to do?

To attack the grizzly bear, turn to page 121.

To run from the grizzly bear, turn to page 96.

Your master calls again. His voice is like an electric shock. You spring to your feet and run up the bank, ahead of the men, to the point of your last departure.

Again the rope is attached. You launch—but this time straight into the stream. Hans pays out the rope, permitting no slack, while Pete keeps it clear of coils. You hold your course until you are on a line straight up river of Thornton. Then you turn and with the speed of a train head down upon him. You strike Thornton like a battering ram, with the whole force of the current behind you. He reaches up and closes with both arms around your shaggy neck.

Hans yanks the rope around a tree, and you and Thornton are jerked under the water. Strangling and suffocating, smashing against rocks and snags, you veer into the bank. You and your master are saved.

Thornton comes to, belly downward. His first glance is for you. Thornton is bruised and battered. He touches carefully all over your body, finding three broken ribs. "That settles it," he announces. "We camp right here."

And camp you do, until your ribs mend and you are able to travel.

That winter, at Dawson, John Thornton enters a conversation in which men boast of their favorite dogs. You, because of your record, are the target of the men. Thornton is driven to defend you. At the end of half an hour, one man states that his dog could start a sled with 500 pounds and walk off with it. A second brags 600 for his dog, and a third brags 700.

"Pooh! pooh!" says John Thornton. "Buck can start 1,000 pounds."

"And break it out? And walk off with it for 100 yards?" demands one of the men, Matthewson.

"And break it out, and walk off with it for 100 yards," John Thornton says coolly.

Matthewson replies, "I've got a thousand dollars that says he can't." He slams a sack of gold upon the bar.

Nobody speaks. A flush of warm blood creeps up your master's face. He does not know whether you can start 1,000 pounds. Half a ton! The eyes of a dozen men fix upon him, silent and waiting. Furthermore, John Thornton has no thousand dollars.

"I've got a sled outside now, with twenty 50-pound sacks of flour on it," Matthewson says.

Thornton does not reply. He glances from face to face in the absent way of a man who has lost the power of thought.

The face of Jim O'Brien, an old-time friend, catches his eyes. "Can you lend me a thousand?" Thornton asks, almost in a whisper.

"Sure," answers O'Brien, thumping down a sack by the side of Matthewson's. "But it's little faith I'm having, John, that the beast can do the trick."

A crowd gathers in the street to see the test. Dealers and gamekeepers come forth to see the outcome of the wager. Several hundred men, furred and mittened, bank around the sled within easy distance.

Matthewson's sled, loaded with 1,000 pounds of flour, has been standing for a couple of hours. In the intense cold the sled's runners have frozen fast to the hard-packed snow. Men offer odds of two to one that you cannot budge the sled.

A quibble arises concerning the meaning of "break out." O'Brien argues it is Thornton's privilege to knock the runners loose, leaving you to "break it out" from a dead standstill. Matthewson insists that the phrase includes breaking the runners from the frozen grip of the snow. A majority of the men who witnessed the bet decide in his favor, and the odds go up to three to one against you.

There are no takers.

Not a man believes you are capable of the feat. Thornton has been hurried into the wager, heavy with doubt. Now that he looks at the sled, the task appears even more impossible.

"Three to one!" Matthewson proclaims. "I would bet another thousand at that figure, Thornton. What do you say?"

Thornton calls Hans and Pete to him. Their money sacks are slim. The three can rake together only 200 dollars. This sum is their total fortunes.

Thornton does what he should have done from the very beginning. He turns to you and asks, "What do you think, Buck? Can you do it?"

It is no minor question. Your master and his friends need more money to continue on their journey. If you answer yes and succeed, they will win the bet and have that money. But if you answer yes and fail, they will likely live the rest of their lives in debt, never leaving Dawson, never having anything of their own. At least, if you answer no, they will cut their losses; their debt will not be so great. Is your answer yes? Or is it no? What will you choose to do?

If you think you can pull the sled, turn to page 74.

If you don't believe you can do it, turn to page 132.

THE END

YOU HAVE ANSWERED THE CALL OF THE WILD!

Turn to page 156.

The risk is worth the reward. A meal of fresh meat awaits, and you intend to have it. You growl low and guttural, and you bare your fangs.

The grizzly takes your bait; she continues her charge. At the last instant, you leap out of her path, slashing her side with your claws.

The grizzly whirls and again rushes. And again you do your trick, slashing her side a second time. You are quicker and wiser than your foe. Or so you think.

The grizzly charges a third time, but she has learned her lesson. This time, as you leap and slash, the bear reaches out with her massive paw. Speed is no match for strength. She swats, and you are flung backward.

You slam into a tree with the force of a moving car. You bounce to the ground with a thud. When you try to push yourself up, you find that you cannot move.

The grizzly leaps upon you. You hear a frenzied snarl and see a flash of white teeth. But you feel no pain. You feel nothing at all. And as you close your eyes for the final time, you are grateful, at least, for that.

Turn to page 73.

Your instincts scream their warnings, but the man in the red sweater taught you a lesson you'll never forget. Death may await you farther along your journey, but death will surely come if you do not obey your master. The command to mush is given, and that is exactly what you do.

You press forward, and your team comes to life. Together, you drive ahead, pulling the sled and your masters. A few moments pass, and John Thornton's camp is but a memory.

You're no more than a mile on your way, when the sound of cracking ice suddenly fills your ears. And by the time you hear the noise, you know it's already too late. The ice crumbles beneath your feet, and you are unwillingly pulled into the deadly hole in the ice.

You are greeted by a stabbing pain. The cold water bites like a million tiny insects. Your first instinct is to cry out, and as you do, you swallow a mouthful of the icy water. You fight to keep your head afloat. Yet any chance of survival ends when the sled plunges into the water behind you.

Your harness pulls tightly against you. You stretch your mouth and nose upward, struggling for one last gasp of air. The strain is too great. You are pulled to the river's bottom, where you struggle in vain to get yourself free.

You hold your breath, still pushing upward with all of your might. But, too quickly, the last of your breath runs out. Panic and instinct take over. You inhale one final time. Your lungs fill with water, spelling the end of an all too short life. The river is now your final resting place.

Turn to page 73.

You spring into the river. At the end of 300 yards, amid a mad swirl of water, you reach Thornton. When you feel him grasp your tail, you paddle for the bank, swimming with all your splendid strength. But the progress shoreward is slow, the progress downstream amazingly rapid. From below comes the fatal roaring where the wild current goes wilder.

The suck of the water is frightful. Thornton scrapes over a rock, bruises across a second, strikes a third with crushing force. He clutches its slippery top with both of his hands, releasing you.

Above the roar of water, he shouts, "Go, Buck! Go!"

When you hear his order, you turn toward the bank. You swim powerfully and are dragged ashore by Pete.

A man can cling to a slippery rock in the face of a driving current for only a matter of minutes. So you run as fast as you can up the bank, to a point far above where Thornton is hanging on.

Hans and Pete attach a line to your neck and shoulders, being careful that it should not strangle you. Again, you launch into the stream. You swim boldly, but not straight enough. You discover the mistake too late. When Thornton is a bare half-dozen strokes away, you are carried helplessly past him.

Hans pulls the rope, thus tightening on you in the sweep of the current. You are jerked under the surface, and under the surface you remain until your body strikes against the bank and you are hauled out.

You are half drowned. You stagger to your feet and fall down. The faint sound of Thornton's voice comes to you. You cannot make out the words of it, but you understand that he's in trouble.

Your first attempts at saving him almost drowned you, and you have lost most of your energy. Another trip into the river might very well finish you off. But he is your master. Should you risk your life with one more try? Or should you rest, trusting that the humans will find a way to save him? What will you choose to do?

To swim to your master again, turn to page 115.

To wait and watch, turn to page 85.

As cunning and skilled a hunter as you are, you are no match for a full-grown moose. You continue on your way, leaving the moose and its band no wiser of your silent presence.

Rested and strong, you turn your face toward camp and Thornton. You break into the long easy lope, and go on, hour after hour, heading straight home. As you walk, you become more and more aware of the new stir in the land. There is life in it, different from the life that has been there through summer. The birds talk of it, the squirrels chatter about it, the very breeze whispers of it.

You arrive at camp and leap upon your master, as is your traditional greeting. You lick his face, bite his hand and gleefully wrestle him to the ground. You remain by his side for days on end, content to spend every hour with the master you love.

One lazy afternoon, you catch a strange scent in the air. It brings with it a feeling of wonder and dread. As sudden as a crack of thunder, you hear the terrifying, unified battle cry of men. You leap to your feet and see a dozen Yeehat warriors charging toward your camp.

Your master is in danger; that is all you need to know. Instinct takes over; you meet the invaders' attack. Arrows fly around you. Nig is struck by one. You do not stop. You are a live hurricane of fury, hurling yourself upon them in a frenzy. You plunge into their midst, tearing, rending, destroying. In constant and terrific motion, you dodge the arrows they discharge at you.

But eventually one finds its mark. An arrow pierces your side, the force of its blow knocking you off your feet. The pain is intense but fleeting. Your body burns, as if on fire, before growing completely numb.

You see John Thornton charging toward you, his face wearing an expression of deep pain and regret. Even before he reaches you, your vision blurs; your eyes fall out of focus. You close them, and a soft whimper escapes your lips. It is the last sound you ever make.

Turn to page 73.

You roar. Your body rises up in the air as you leave the floor for Burton's throat. The man is hurled backward to the floor with you on top of him. You drive in again for the throat. The man succeeds only in partly blocking you.

Then the crowd is upon you, and you are driven off. A miners' meeting is called. The group decides that you had good reason to attack, and you are released.

But your reputation is made. From that day, your name spreads through every camp in Alaska.

Turn to the next page.

Later on, in the fall, Thornton and his partners must guide a long and narrow poling-boat down a bad stretch of rapids. Hans and Pete move along the bank. John Thornton remains in the boat, helping it along by means of a pole and shouting directions to the shore. On the bank, you watch anxiously, your eyes never off your master.

At a particularly bad spot, the boat smashes into the bank. Thornton is flung out of it and carried downstream toward the worst part of the rapids.

His life is in danger. He could drown. Can Thornton save himself? Or does he need your help? You might be the only thing that can rescue him. Or you might make the situation worse, putting your own life at risk, causing your master to worry about you when he should be saving himself. Will you jump in? Or will you wait on the shore? What will you choose to do?

To swim to your master, turn to page 124.

To wait and watch, turn to page 94.

A moment's pause falls, and you remain motionless as a statue. Then the boldest one leaps straight for you. Like a flash you strike, bringing him down. Then you stand, without movement, as before. Three others try it; and one after the other they draw back, bleeding from the slashes caused by you.

This is enough to fling the whole pack forward. You are marvelously quick and agile. Pivoting on your hind legs, and snapping and gashing, you are everywhere at once. You present a front, which is unbroken as you whirl and guard from side to side. But to prevent them from getting behind you, you are forced back into the creek bed, till you stand against a high gravel bank. Here, you come to bay, protected on three sides and with nothing to do but face the front.

And you face it well. At the end of half an hour, the wolves draw back in defeat. The tongues of all are out and lolling, the white fangs showing in the moonlight. Some are lying down with heads raised and ears pricked forward. Others stand on their feet, watching you. Still others are lapping water from the pool. One wolf, long and lean and gray, advances cautiously, in a friendly manner. You recognize the wild brother with whom you had run for a night and a day. He whines softly, and you touch noses.

An old wolf, gaunt and battle-scarred, comes forward. You sniff noses with him. The old wolf sits down, points nose at the moon, and breaks out the long wolf howl. The others sit down and howl. And now the call comes to you. You, too, sit and howl.

This over, the pack crowds around you, sniffing in half-friendly, half-savage manner. The leaders spring away into the woods. The wolves swing in behind, yelping in chorus. And you run with them, side by side with the wild brother, yelping as you run.

Turn to page 88.

You would give your life for John Thornton, and you would never hope to disappoint him. Yet, in your heart of hearts, you know he is asking too much. It breaks your spirit to do so, but you look down, turning your head away. The meaning is obvious; your answer is no.

Thornton releases you. He forces a smile and pats your head. You whimper softly.

He nods and says, "It's okay, Buck."

But it isn't okay. Your master and his friends are nearly out of money. They haven't enough to go back, and they haven't enough to continue forward. They are stuck here—and you with them.

Had Thornton taken the bet and had you won it, your troubles would be over. You would be on your way to a new life, a better existence.

Instead, you must remain here, possibly forever. You have disappointed the only human you've ever loved. You have left him trapped, an arm's reach from his life's dream. Because of you, he may never attain it.

Turn to the next page.

Thornton walks away, head down, shoulders slunked. You follow as he trudges back to camp. The man looks sad and defeated, and his sunken mood is your fault.

Will you ever be able to forgive yourself for this great disappointment? It's a question that you will have the rest of your life to consider.

Turn to page 73.

More tired than you have ever felt before, you do something you thought you'd never do. You refuse your master. It is not only for yourself that you make this desperate stand. It is for the team that follows you. The lash bites into you, but you neither whine nor struggle.

Your master exchanges whip for club. You refuse to move. Like your mates, you are barely able to get up. But, unlike them, you have made up your mind not to get up. You refuse to stir. You have already suffered so greatly, and now you feel strangely numb.

The last sensations of pain leave you. You no longer feel anything. And in the end, your master curses you a final time. He hurries back to the sled to retrieve a new weapon, and you understand that your life is at an end.

Turn to page 73.

The wolf ceases from its howling and tries to sense your presence. Your choice made, you stalk into the open, half crouching, tail straight and stiff, feet falling with care. Every movement advertises friendliness.

The wolf flees. You follow, with wild leapings, in a frenzy to overtake. You run him into a blind channel, in the bed of the creek where a timber jam blocks the way. The wolf whirls, snarling and bristling. He clips his teeth together.

You do not attack. You circle him about and hedge him in with friendly advances. The wolf is suspicious and afraid. You make three of him in weight, while his head barely reaches your shoulder. Watching for his chance, he darts away. The chase resumes.

Time and again he is cornered, and the chain of events repeats. He runs until your head is even with his flank. He whirls around at bay, only to dash away again at the first opportunity.

But in the end, you are rewarded. The wolf, finding that no harm is intended, finally sniffs noses with you. Then you become friendly, and you play about in a nervous way. After some time, the wolf starts off in a manner that shows he is going somewhere. He makes it clear that you are to come. So you run side by side through the twilight, straight up the creek bed, into the gorge, and across the divide.

You are wildly glad. You are answering the call, running by the side of your wood brother toward the place from where the call surely comes. You are running free, earth underfoot, the wide sky overhead.

You stop by a stream to drink, and you remember John Thornton. You sit. The wolf starts on, then returns to you, sniffing noses and making actions to encourage you. But you turn around and start slowly back.

For the better part of an hour, the wild brother runs by your side, whining softly. Then he sits down, points his nose upward, and howls a mournful howl. As you hold steadily on your way, you hear it grow fainter until it is lost.

John Thornton is eating dinner when you dash into camp. You spring upon him in a frenzy of affection, licking his face and biting his hand. For two days and nights you never leave camp, never let Thornton out of your sight. You follow him at his work, watch him while he eats, see him into his blankets at night and out of them in the morning.

But after two days, the call in the forest begins to sound more powerfully than ever. Your restlessness comes back. You are haunted by memories of the wild brother and of the smiling land beyond the divide.

Once again, you take to wandering in the woods, but the wild brother comes no more. You listen, but the mournful howl is never raised.

You begin to sleep out at night, staying away from camp for days at a time. Once, you cross the divide at the head of the creek, and you go down into the land of timber and streams. There you wander for a week, seeking fresh sign of the wild brother but finding none.

You fish for salmon in a broad stream. By this stream you kill a large black bear. It is a hard fight, and it arouses your ferocity. Two days later, you return to your kill and find a dozen wolverines quarrelling over the spoil. You chase them off, downing two of them in the process.

The longing becomes stronger. You are a thing that preys, living on things that live, alone, surviving in a hostile environment. You possess great pride in yourself. From your Saint Bernard father, you inherited size and weight, but it was your shepherd mother who gave shape to that size and weight. Your muzzle is the long wolf muzzle—but larger than the muzzle of any wolf. Your head is the wolf head on a massive scale. Your cunning is wolf cunning, and it is wild cunning. Your intelligence is shepherd intelligence and Saint Bernard intelligence. All this, plus an experience gained in the fiercest of schools, makes you as formidable a creature as any that roam the wild.

"Never was there such a dog," says John Thornton one day, as the partners watch you move.

They see you march out of camp, but they do not see the instant transformation within the secrecy of the forest. At once you become a thing of the wild, a passing shadow that appears and disappears among the shadows. You know how to take advantage of every cover, to crawl on your belly like a snake, to leap and strike. You can take a bird from its nest, kill a rabbit as it sleeps, and snap the little chipmunks fleeing a second too late for the trees. Fish, in open pools, are not too quick for you. You kill to eat, and you prefer to eat what you kill yourself.

As the fall of the year comes, the moose appear in greater abundance. You wish strongly for large and formidable quarry, and you come upon it one day at the head of the creek. A band of 20 moose have crossed over from the land of streams and timber. A great bull moose is chief among them.

The bull moose is very large and powerful—more powerful than anything you've ever fought before. He stands over six feet tall and is in a savage temper. You long for the challenge, but is it a challenge worth taking? Is the game worth the risk of life and limb? You must decide. Should you attack the bull moose? Or should you leave it be? What will you choose to do?

To hunt the moose, turn to page 152.

To sneak away from the moose, turn to page 126.

Your decision made, you give no effort to rise. You lie quietly. The lash bites into you, but you neither whine nor struggle. Several times Thornton starts, as though to speak, but changes his mind. A moisture comes into his eyes. As the whipping continues, he arises and begins to pace.

Hal exchanges whip for club. You refuse to move. Like your mates, you are barely able to get up. But, unlike them, you have made up your mind not to get up. You have a feeling of impending doom. This has been strong upon you since you pulled into the bank. What of the thin and rotten ice you have felt under your feet all day? You sense disaster close at hand, out there ahead on the ice where your master is trying to drive you.

You refuse to stir. You have already suffered so much that the blows do not hurt. And as they continue to fall upon you, you feel strangely numb. The last sensations of pain leave you. You no longer feel anything, though very faintly you can hear the impact of the club upon your body.

And then, without warning, Thornton utters a cry that is like the cry of an animal. He springs upon the man.

Hal is hurled backward, as though struck by a falling tree. Mercedes screams. Charles looks on and wipes his watery eyes, but he does not get up.

John Thornton stands over you, struggling madly to control himself, too angry to speak. "If you strike that dog again, it'll be the last thing you do," he at last manages to say.

"It's my dog," Hal replies. "Get out of my way, or I'll fix you. I'm going to Dawson."

Thornton stands between him and you. Hal draws his long hunting-knife. Mercedes screams. Thornton raps Hal's knuckles with the axe-handle, knocking the knife to the ground. He raps his knuckles again as Hal tries to pick it up. Then Thornton stoops, picks it up himself, and cuts you out of your traces.

Hal has no fight left in him. A few minutes later they pull out from the bank and down the river. You hear them go and raise your head to see: Pike is leading, Sol-leks is at the wheel, and between are Joe and Teek. They are limping. Mercedes is riding the loaded sled. Hal guides at the gee-pole, and Charles stumbles along in the rear.

As you watch them, Thornton kneels beside you. With rough, kindly hands, he searches for broken bones. His search reveals nothing more than many bruises and a state of terrible starvation.

The sled is a quarter of a mile away. You and he watch it crawl along over the ice. Suddenly, you see its back end drop down, as into a rut. Mercedes' scream comes to your ears. You see Charles turn and make one step to run back, and then a whole section of ice gives way. Dogs and humans disappear. A yawning hole is all that can be seen. The bottom has dropped out of the trail.

Thornton looks at you. "You poor devil," he says.

You lick his hand.

Turn to the next page.

6
FOR THE LOVE OF A MAN

"When I froze my feet last December," Thornton tells you, "my partners made me comfortable and then left for Dawson."

He was still limping slightly at the time he rescued you. But with the continued warm weather, even the slight limp has left him. Here, lying by the river bank through the long spring days, you watch the running water. You listen lazily to the songs of birds and the hum of nature. You slowly win back your strength.

A rest comes very good after traveling 3,000 miles. Your wounds heal, your muscles swell out, and the flesh comes back to cover your bones. You are all loafing—you, John Thornton, and his dogs, Skeet and Nig—

waiting for the raft to come that will carry you down to Dawson.

Skeet is a little Irish setter who easily made friends with you. She has the compassion of a doctor, which some dogs possess. And as a mother cat washes her kittens, she has washed and cleaned your wounds. Nig, equally friendly, is a huge black dog, half bloodhound and half deerhound, with a good nature.

These dogs show no jealousy toward you. They seem to share the kindness of John Thornton. As you grow stronger, they entice you into all sorts of ridiculous games. Thornton himself joins; and in this fashion, you romp into a new life. Love, genuine passionate love, is yours for the first time. This you never experienced at Judge Miller's. With the Judge it had been a friendship. But love that is feverish and burning, that is adoration, it has taken John Thornton to arouse.

This man saved your life, which is something. But, further, he is the ideal master. Other men see to the welfare of their dogs from a sense of duty and business; he sees to his as if they are his own children, because he cannot help it.

To sit down for a long talk with you is as much his delight as yours. He has a way of taking your head roughly between his hands and resting his own head upon yours. He shakes you back and forth, calling you names that to you are love names.

You know no greater joy than that rough embrace. At each jerk back and forth, your joy is so great that it seems your heart will be shaken out of your body. And when released, you spring to your feet, your mouth laughing without movement.

John Thornton exclaims, "You can all but speak!"

You show your love expression by seizing Thornton's hand in your mouth and closing so that the flesh bears the imprint of your teeth. The man understands this bite for love.

For a long time after your rescue, you do not like John Thornton to get out of your sight. You are afraid that he will pass out of your life as Perrault, Francois and the Scotch have. Even in the night, in your dreams, you are haunted by this fear. At such times you creep to the flap of his tent, where you stand and listen to the sound of his breathing.

In spite of this great love, the strain of the primitive, which the Northland has aroused in you, remains alive and active. Faithfulness and devotion are yours, yet you retain your wildness.

Because of your very great love, you cannot steal from this man. But from any other man, in any other camp, you do not hesitate. Your face and body are scored by the teeth of many dogs, and you fight as fiercely as ever. Skeet and Nig belong to John Thornton, so you do not quarrel with them. But with any other dogs, you are merciless. You have learned well the law of club and fang. You must rule or be ruled, eat or be eaten.

Deep in the forest, a call sounds. It is thrilling and luring. You feel compelled to plunge into the forest, and on and on. But every time you do so, your love for John Thornton draws you back to him again.

Thornton alone holds you. When his partners, Hans and Pete, arrive on the long-expected raft, you refuse to notice them until you learn they are close to Thornton.

"That dog will do anything for you," Pete declares, nodding his head toward you. "I'm not hankering to be the man that picks a fight with you while he's around."

It is at Circle City that Pete's worries are realized. Black Burton, a man evil-tempered and mean, picks a quarrel with a young man at the bar. Thornton steps between to stop the fight before it begins.

You, as is your custom, lie in a corner, head on paws, watching your master's every action. Burton strikes, without warning. John Thornton is sent spinning and saves himself from falling only by clutching the rail of the bar.

Your master has just been punched. Whether he likes it or not, he's in a fight. He might get seriously hurt—or worse. You are loyal to him, and you want to come to his aid. But any dog who attacks a person is almost always put to death. Should you help Thornton? Should you stay in the corner? What will you choose to do?

To attack Burton, turn to page 128.

To stay in the corner and watch, turn to page 150.

147

Humans with weapons are best left unprovoked. Your life's experiences have taught you that. Despite the gust of overpowering rage that sweeps over you, you silently slink away from the desolated camp.

John Thornton is probably dead, but you do not know this for certain. The lack of knowledge will haunt you for the rest of your days. It leaves a great void in you, somewhat akin to hunger. It is a void which aches and aches and which food cannot fill.

Night comes on, and a full moon rises high over the trees into the sky. And with the coming of the night, you become alive to a stirring of the new life in the forest. You stand up, listening and scenting. From far away drifts a faint, sharp yelp, followed by a chorus of similar sharp yelps. The yelps grow closer and louder.

Turn to the next page.

You walk to the center of an open space and listen. It is the call, the many-noted call, sounding more luring than ever before. And you are finally ready to obey.

Hunting their living meat, the wolf pack has at last crossed over from the land of streams and timber. They pour into the clearing where the moonlight streams, and in the center of the clearing you wait.

The wolves glare at you, making their intentions clear. They mean to attack. Are you strong enough to stand against an entire wolf pack? Or will doing so be the end of you? Is it wiser to escape and to ensure your lonely freedom elsewhere in this rugged land? Or will you stand your ground? What will you choose to do?

To run from the wolves, turn to page 86.

To stay where you are, turn to page 130.

Your master is good and strong and brave. He can take care of himself. You remain in the corner, watching intently as the fight unfolds.

Thornton regains his balance and rubs the left side of his chin, where Burton's fist met his face. Your master is willing to forgive Burton's assault, but he is not given the chance. Burton springs upon him and continues the attack.

This time, Thornton is not caught unprepared. He puts up a worthy fight—ducking, dodging and blocking Burton's fists with his forearms. He lands a few punches of his own, and the battle shifts in your master's favor.

Thornton lands another punch and another. Then he steps back to see if his opponent is ready to quit. But Burton is a cruel man, ruled by his emotions. In the heat of the moment, he makes a rash decision. The pause in the action allows him to reach into his pocket.

A moment too late, you realize what is about to happen. You jump to your feet as Burton pulls out a sharp object. He lunges toward Thornton. His blade sinks into your master—and a long, heartbreaking howl escapes your lips.

John Thornton slumps to the ground, stabbed. Your heart stings as if you were pierced by the blade. Your master is dead, and you feel suddenly certain that you could have saved him.

The pain of his loss is so great that it drives you onto the floor beside him. You collapse, pressing your eyes closed. Your world has lost all meaning. You have no reason to carry on. What will you do? Where will you go? The answer escapes you, for you do not yet know your true nature. And because of that, you will live the rest of your life lost and alone.

Turn to page 73.

This is the ultimate test of skill; you will not pass it up. You leap forward and bark, announcing your presence. Back and forth the bull moose tosses his great antlers, which branch to 14 points and seven feet apart. His small eyes burn with a bitter light, and he roars with fury at the sight of you.

You cut the bull out from the herd. You bark and dance in front of the bull. You remain just out of reach of the great antlers and terrible hoofs, which could stamp your life out with a single blow. Unable to turn his back on you, the bull is driven into moments of rage. At such moments he charges, and you retreat, luring him on.

As twilight falls, the old bull stands with lowered head, watching his herd as they shamble away. He can not follow, for you are a merciless fanged terror that will not let him go. More than half a ton he weighs; he has lived a long, strong life, full of fight and struggle. Yet at the end, he faces death at the teeth of a creature whose head does not reach beyond his knees.

From then on, night and day, you never leave your prey, never give it a moment's rest. You never permit it to eat—nor do you give the bull opportunity to quench his burning thirst in the streams he crosses. Often, in desperation, he bursts into long stretches of flight. At such times, you lope easily at his heels, satisfied with the way the game is played. You lie down when the moose stands still, attacking him fiercely when he tries to eat or drink.

The great head droops more and more under its tree of horns; the shambling trot grows weak and weaker. He takes to standing for long periods, with nose to the ground and ears dropped limply. You find more time to get water for yourself and to rest.

At such moments, it appears to you that a change is coming over the face of things. You can feel a new stir in the land. As the moose are coming into the land, other kinds of life are coming in. The news of it comes to you, not by sight, or sound, or smell, but by some other sense. You hear nothing and see nothing, yet you know that the land is somehow different. Strange things are afoot and ranging; you must investigate after you finish the business in hand.

At last, at the end of the fourth day, you pull the great moose down. For a day and a night you remain by the kill, eating and sleeping. Then, rested and strong, you turn your face toward camp and Thornton. You break into the long easy lope, and go on, hour after hour, heading straight home.

As you walk, you become more and more aware of the new stir in the land. There is life in it, different from the life that has been there through the summer. The birds talk of it, the squirrels chatter about it, the very breeze whispers of it. Several times you stop and draw in the fresh morning air in great sniffs. You read a message which makes you leap on with greater speed. You are overwhelmed with a sense of dread. As you cross the last watershed and drop into the valley toward camp, you proceed with greater caution.

Three miles away, you come upon a fresh trail that sends your neck hair bristling. It leads straight toward camp and John Thornton. You hurry on, swiftly and stealthily, every nerve straining and tense. You remark the silence of the forest. The birds have flitted away. The squirrels are in hiding.

As you slide along, your nose jerks suddenly. You follow the new scent into a thicket and find Nig. He is lying on his side, an arrow in his body. A hundred yards farther on, you come upon one of the sled-dogs. He, too, is dead. You pass around him without stopping.

From the camp comes the faint sound of many voices. Bellying forward to the edge of the clearing, you find Hans, lying on his face, feathered with arrows. You peer out and see what makes your hair leap straight up on your neck and shoulders: A band of Yeehat Indians are dancing about the wreckage of your camp.

You are consumed by two equal and opposing thoughts: fight or flee. The men are armed, and they outnumber you. You stand little chance against them. Yet revenge is a great motivator. Should you attack? Or should you return to the forest forever? What will you choose to do?

To attack the Yeehats, turn to page 101.

To return to the forest, turn to page 148.

ABOUT JACK LONDON

Jack London was born in San Francisco in 1876. He loved to read and began his writing career by sending stories, jokes, and poems to many different publications. More often than not, his work was turned down.

He spent the winter of 1897 in the Yukon during the gold rush, using his experiences to write *The Call of the Wild* in 1903. The story made him famous.

Mr. London went on to write dozens of other books, including *White Fang* and *The Sea-Wolf.* He is also well known for his short stories, essays, and plays.

London died from kidney failure on November 22, 1916. Nearly 100 years later, he is still considered one of the best writers in U.S. history.

ABOUT THE CALL OF THE WILD

Before Jack London's *The Call of the Wild* was a book, it appeared as a series in a popular magazine. *The Saturday Evening Post* printed the story, in five parts, in 1903.

Mr. London wrote the story based on his experiences in Alaska; he was a prospector during the gold rush in the winter of 1897. Many people believe that the story is popular because it is so realistic and that the story is so realistic because London lived through similar events.

After *The Call of the Wild* appeared in *The Saturday Evening Post,* a longer version was published as a book, later that same year. It catapulted London into international stardom.

This version of Mr. London's classic work condenses his novel. It is with great respect for Mr. London that we present his timeless tale as a choose your path book.

CAN YOU SURVIVE

Test your survival skills with a free
short story at www.Lake7Creative.com

and pick up these
Choose Your Path books:

YOU'RE THE MAIN CHARACTER. YOU MAKE THE CHOICES.
CAN YOU SURVIVE?

SIR ARTHUR CONAN DOYLE'S
ADVENTURES OF
SHERLOCK
HOLMES

YOU'RE THE MAIN CHARA
CAN YO

JACK LON

CA
W

THESE STORIES?

Jack London's
Call of the Wild

Jules Verne's
20,000 Leagues Under the Sea

Sir Arthur Conan Doyle's
Adventures of Sherlock Holmes

YOU'RE THE MAIN CHARACTER. YOU MAKE THE CHOICES.
CAN YOU SURVIVE?

Jules Verne's
20,000 LEAGUES UNDER THE SEA

MAKE THE CHOICES.
IVE?

OF THE
LD

ABOUT RYAN JACOBSON

Ryan Jacobson has always loved choose your path books, so he is thrilled to get a chance to write them. He used his memories of those fun-filled stories and his past experiences to write *Lost in the Wild*. The book became so popular that he followed it with *Storm at the Summit of Mount Everest* and *Can You Survive: Jack London's Call of the Wild*.

Ryan is the author of nearly 20 books, including picture books, comics, graphic novels, chapter books and ghost stories. He lives in Mora, Minnesota, with his wife Lora, sons Jonah and Lucas, and dog Boo.

For more details, visit RyanJacobsonOnline.com.